*Praise for Elizabeth Engstrom*

### On *How to Write a Sizzling Sex Scene*:

"All writers could benefit from reading this book, whether they're writing erotica or not. Fun to read and insightful. This book clearly shows how sex and sensuality can add zest and depth to any character's story."

—Alexis Duran, author of the *Masters and Mages* and *Edges of Night* erotic fantasy series

### On *Black Leather*:

A darkly seductive page-turner by a writer who knows how to put the erotic thrill into a thriller.

—*DarkEcho*

An artfully written and highly recommended erotic and psychological suspense from first page to last.

—*Midwest Book Review*

### On *Suspicions*:

This is where she's at her best.

—*Locus*

A spooky collection of tales.

—*Publishers Weekly*

"Like many fine writers, Engstrom's stories are across all genres. Some can be termed sf, others as mystery or fantasy or horror, still others are simply "fiction." A few are light and humorous. Most are quietly dark, slightly skewed, angled toward that indescribable place just at the edge of shadow. All are worth reading. Many are worth pondering. By the end, at least one suspicion will definitely be confirmed: Elizabeth Engstrom is one of the best. No doubts."

—*Cemetery Dance*

On **Lizzie Borden**:
Every door in the Borden house is metaphorically locked, and each room holds the terrible secrets of the occupant... Engstrom [moves] the reader inexorably toward the anticipated savage denouement.

*—Publishers Weekly*

Engstrom has woven a fascinating tale of a lonely, tormented and frustrated young woman.

*—Rocky Mountain News*

A real page-turner and white-knuckler. The tension mounts without letup.

*—Maui News*

Engstrom crafts a character with motivation, mental confusion and smoldering resentment, a woman who could stand unblinking in a shower of blood as she bludgeoned her parents to death.

*—Ogden Standard Examiner*

On **Lizard Wine**:
"*Lizard Wine* is the book your mother warned you about, sleek, nasty, perfectly focused, smart as hell, absolutely convincing, and utterly single-minded."

—Peter Straub, author of *Ghost Story*

"Excruciating suspense!"

—Bryce Courtenay, author of *The Power of One*

Supertaut storytelling.

*—Kirkus Reviews*

On **When Darkness Loves Us**:
A masterpiece, and one of the finest tragedies I've read in years.

*—Horror Show*

"Behind that soft-voiced style is power, is surprise, is... ferocity."

—Theodore Sturgeon

# Books by Elizabeth Engstrom

## Novels
*When Darkness Loves Us*
*Black Ambrosia*
*Lizzie Borden*
*Lizard Wine*
*Black Leather*
*Candyland*
*The Northwoods Chronicles*
*York's Moon*
*Baggage Check*

## Collections of Short Fiction
*Nightmare Flower*
*The Alchemy of Love*
*Suspicions*

## Nonfiction Books
*Something Happened to Grandma*
*How to Write a Sizzling Sex Scene*

## Anthologies Edited
*Word by Word* (co-editor)
*Imagination Fully Dilated* (co-editor)
*Imagination Fully Dilated vol. II* (editor)
*Dead on Demand* (editor)
*Pronto! Writings from Rome* (co-editor)
*Ship's Log: Writings at Sea* (co-editor)
*Lies and Limericks* (co-editor)
*Mota 9: Addiction* (editor)

# Baggage Check

by Elizabeth Engstrom

IFD Publishing
P.O. Box 40776, Eugene, Oregon 97404 U.S.A.
www.ifdpublishing.com

Copyright © 2015 Elizabeth Engstrom
Cover Art, Copyright © Alan M. Clark 2015
ISBN: 978-0-9965536-4-3
Originally Printed in the United States of America

This book is dedicated to past mistakes and all the heartaches that came with them, as well as to future joys and all those heartaches which will surely come.

# Baggage Check

## by Elizabeth Engstrom

Publishing
Eugene, Oregon

# Chapter One

*One Friday Evening*

Even though Sweetann Holt hardly ever used her luggage, she knew what it looked like of course, and knew immediately that the suitcase standing at the end of the bed in her brother's guest room wasn't hers.

After a thin dinner of probably only two hundred calories that she was sure Natalie had prepared to show her how to eat properly, Sweetann had gone up to the room that she would use for the weekend. She had some red licorice stashed, knowing that it'd come in handy while under her sister-in-law's watchful eye.

But when she saw where Richard had put her suitcase, she knew it wasn't hers. She looked at it, frowned, then being the efficient working single mom that she was, automatically began to calculate all the implications: 1. Where was her suitcase? 2. When was she going to get it back? 3. Who was going to find it and return it for her? 4. Was this going to mess up her weekend? 5. Was there anything in it that she couldn't live without? Besides, of course, the red licorice.

Sweetann decided that she could buy a few extra pairs of undies and a toothbrush. She didn't need much for the two days she'd be in Los Angeles. This snafu didn't have to ruin their weekend. Or worse, consume the weekend.

The weekend was already being consumed by the news that their parents had died with more debt than assets. Sweetann had counted on at least a little inheritance to help her over her current financial situation.

She intended to investigate very carefully the numbers that Richard had given her. She didn't trust Richard's wife—if anybody could loot their parents' estate and justify it, it would be Natalie, but spineless Richard would stand right next to her while she did it.

Confident that the news about the suitcase was not terribly bad, she went out and stood at the top of the stairs.

"I'm sorry, but I think we have a little problem," she

announced to Natalie and Richard, who were sitting on their silk chenille sofa sipping their expensive after-dinner wine. They both looked up at her.

"This isn't my suitcase."

"No," Richard said, disbelief on his face. "I picked up the wrong suitcase?"

Sweetann shrugged. "Looks like."

He took the stairs two at a time, and breezed past her into the bedroom. Natalie gave her an exasperated "Men!" look, smiled, then got up and slowly ascended the stairs. Natalie moved like a model, skinny as an x-ray, something that had always annoyed Sweetann, and annoyed her all over again. Natalie always looked lithe and feline, something Sweetann would never be.

"I'm sure I've got anything you need," she purred as she passed Sweetann. But Sweetann knew that she'd never fit into any of Natalie's size one clothes, and Sweetann knew that Natalie knew it, too.

Sweetann curled her lip, said a quiet "Thanks," then followed her into the bedroom to join in the discussion of remedy.

Sweetann had tried—really tried—for the whole ten years of Richard's marriage to get over the envy she held for Natalie's style, but hadn't accomplished it yet. Sweetann felt short, stocky and low-class next to Natalie, although she knew she was none of those things.

"You're sure?" Richard asked as he looked over the suitcase. "This isn't the one you pointed at?"

"Mine is pretty much like this one," Sweetann said. "And a million others."

Richard lifted it and set it on the bed. Plain black. Wheels. Heavy. "You're sure."

Sweetann smiled indulgently. "Mine has a big blue name tag from the travel agency. This one doesn't even have an airline claim check."

"Well, we'll just go back to the airport and get yours," Richard said.

The zippers had a blue plastic security tab tying them together. "Give me your pocket knife, Richard," Natalie said, and held out her hand.

Reluctantly, knowing there was no arguing with Natalie, he pulled his pen knife from his pocket, sliced through the plastic tabs and unzipped the suitcase. Natalie flipped the top open.

Sweetann heard herself gasp. Then she heard Natalie gasp. She couldn't believe what she thought she'd seen, but by the time she elbowed her way past Natalie to take a good look, a solid look, a serious look, Richard had closed the suitcase and zipped it. "This goes back to the airport right now," he said.

The three of them stared at the closed suitcase as if struck dumb.

Natalie was the first to awaken. "Wait," she said, putting a finely-manicured hand on Richard's arm. "I think we should talk about this."

"Nope," Richard said. "No discussion. This is trouble. I don't want any trouble."

"It's already trouble," Natalie said. "Taking another look can't be any more trouble." She looked to Sweetann, who nodded, moved in front of Richard, unzipped the top and opened the heavy case.

Sweetann had never seen anything like it. It scared her and it thrilled her. All sorts of possibilities flew through her mind. It could be the answer to so many questions, so many problems, so many situations.

It could be the answer to her prayers.

It could mean a real future. It could mean a decent college for Nicky.

Hell, it could mean a real *present*, never mind a future. She'd been counting on a little inheritance from her folks, spending it on long-neglected necessities before she had it in hand, and now there was no inheritance, thanks to what she suspected were Richard and Natalie's shenanigans.

She had put herself into serious financial trouble, which gave her dark dreams of faceless people chasing her down deserted streets. At times, she couldn't look Nicky in the eye, especially when there was some extra charge for something he wanted to do at school and she didn't have the cash. She clung to her job with a desperation that nobody should ever have to feel, knowing she would do anything they asked, if they just would not fire her. She rotated the bills she could not pay so that everything was paid at least once every three months, but knew that was going to come to a screeching halt some time soon. Very soon. Someone was going to get grumpy and mess up her system, and her whole fragile house of cards would crash.

She had no idea who or what was going to save them, but she felt certain that somehow, someway, something would come along.

And now, out of the blue, it appeared as though something had.

Five minutes later, they were sitting in the living room again, leaning in toward each other conspiratorially. The suitcase, closed and locked, stood sentinel at the foot of the guest room bed where Richard had originally set it.

"Well, we're keeping it," Natalie said. "And that's all there is to that."

"No," Richard said, but it was clear to Sweetann that he could be persuaded. Sweetann had never been entirely certain who wore the pants in this family.

"Well," Sweetann said. "If we're going to keep it, we're going to have to get moving."

"Moving?" Natalie said.

"Snap out of it, kids," Sweetann said. "Whoever got my suitcase instead of that one isn't going to be very happy with old K-Mart underwear and discount deodorant." Sweetann surprised herself with this little speech. But it was clear that the sight of the interior of that suitcase had put Richard and Natalie into some kind of a trance.

"She's right," Richard said, looking at his wife. "The suitcase goes back. I don't want any trouble."

"We're keeping it," Natalie said. "Let's just get moving." She looked at Sweetann. "What's the plan?"

Sweetann almost laughed out loud. They were suddenly co-conspirators and she was the one with the brains. Natalie might be the one with the looks, faded though they were rapidly becoming, but Sweetann had the brains and that wasn't likely to change. "Let's empty the suitcase," she said, "fill it full of old clothes and take it back to the airport, say we got the wrong case, exchange it for the right one, and we'll be on our way."

"Nope," Richard said. "There are bad guys involved here—seriously *bad* bad guys—" he looked at each of them to make certain they got his message "—and they would never swallow such a story. Besides, that suitcase has no claim check on it. This has got to have something to do with airport employees. Smugglers. The Mob."

"How do you know that?" Natalie asked. "Maybe the claim check just fell off."

"Are you kidding me? Did you see what was inside of it?" He looked at Sweetann. "I pulled it right off the luggage carousel. I thought it was the one you pointed at before you left for the ladies' room." He shook his head. "Somebody made a big mistake here, and somebody is going to have to pay for it."

"Not us," Natalie said. "I'm not paying for their criminal incompetence."

"Okay, then. We go back to the airport right now," Sweetann said, pleased to be in the spotlight. She discovered that she liked the new role of Mastermind. "We pick up my suitcase with the claim check. If anybody asks, we say we didn't want to wait for the baggage, so we went out for dinner and are just coming now to pick it up. But nobody will ask; it's none of their business."

"And what about the suitcase upstairs?" Richard asked.

"Never saw it," Sweetann answered.

"Perfect," Natalie said, jumping to her feet. "C'mon, let's go."

~ ~ ~

The baggage claim area at the airport was fairly deserted when they got there. Sweetann and Richard left Natalie in the car in the short term parking lot and went inside.

Sweetann's heart was beating so hard she was panting. She knew her cheeks were red with excitement, and hoped she didn't look like she was trying to get away with something. She had never been good at poker.

She stepped up to the baggage claim counter, pulled out her ticket jacket with the claim stapled inside and when the jumpsuited attendant came over to her, she said, "I'd like to pick up my bag." She pointed behind the desk to her bag, sitting among a half dozen others. "That black one, with the big blue ID tag."

The attendant took her claim check and compared it, then hauled the black bag out and set it on the floor. "Thanks," Sweetann said. Richard pulled out the handle and wheeled it out to the car.

"That was easy," he said under his breath, but a backward glance as they went through the automatic doors gave Sweetann something to worry about.

The baggage attendant was watching them go.

She shouldn't have looked back. She should never have looked back.

Dammit.

~ ~ ~

"We did it!" Natalie whirled in the kitchen when they got back to the house. "We got away with it!" She headed straight to the bottle of wine on the counter and pulled out the cork.

"We haven't gotten away with anything yet," Richard said, taking the bottle from her.

A look passed between them that Sweetann understood. Natalie was trying to control her drinking. She said she wanted a baby—although Sweetann couldn't imagine Natalie changing a diaper—and was limiting herself to an unnatural one glass of wine per day. It was a struggle. She'd been in and out of AA for years, but the best she could do was to keep from poisoning herself while she waited for conception.

Sweetann picked up the kitchen telephone and dialed her house in Seattle. It rang four times and then she heard Nicky's voice. It made her smile.

"Hello?"

"Hi, sweetie."

"Hi, Mom."

"I made it to your Uncle Richard and Aunt Natalie's. Were you sleeping?"

"No, the phone rang a while ago. Woke me up."

"Oh?" That was odd. Her social life didn't include a lot of phone calls, especially not this late on a Friday night.

She felt Richard and Natalie's eyes on her, and resisted the impulse to turn away from them. "Who called?"

"Some guy you work with. William."

Sweetann didn't work with anyone named William. Someone from Human Resources, calling to say she was fired and that she could pick up her final paycheck on Monday morning? "William?" she said, the fear of HR replaced by the fear of a faceless mob guy who was missing a suitcase. "What did he want?"

"He wanted to talk to you, said it was important. I told him you were at Uncle Richard's."

Protective feelings for her ten-year-old son began to burble and churn. "Did you give him the phone number here?"

"Yeah."

"Good boy. Are you all ready for tomorrow?"

"Sort of. I'm still learning my lines."

"You'll be great. It's past your bedtime now, I want you to go to bed and be all rested up for the rehearsal. Let me talk with Charlotte."

"Okay. I love you, Mom."

"Love you too, sweetie. I'll see you Sunday night."

"Okay."

A fumble of the phone and Charlotte's teenage voice came on. "Hello?"

"Hi, Charlotte."

"Oh hi, Mrs. Holt."

"Charlotte, I just wanted you to make sure you know that if anything suspicious happens, you lock yourself and Nicky in one of the upstairs bedrooms and call 911. Don't fool around, okay?"

"I don't like the sound of that," Charlotte said. "Couldn't I just call my mom?"

"Of course," Sweetann said. "We just haven't talked about emergency procedures for a while, and well, this is the first time I've been gone a whole weekend. I just want to make sure you know what to do if anything happens."

"Okay. Don't worry."

"I won't. Just use your good common sense."

"Okay."

"See you Sunday night."

Sweetann wasn't at all sure that Charlotte got the message or that she had good common sense. Homesickness punched her in the chest and she wanted to run home right then to Nicky, but she couldn't do that. Not if they were going to keep that suitcase. If they were going to keep that suitcase—and what was in it—she couldn't do anything out of the ordinary.

And keeping that suitcase was her ticket out of the hand-to-mouth, semi-poverty, escalating, insurmountable debt that Scotty had left her with when he took off nine years ago.

She hung up the phone, then went to the living room where Richard had deposited her real suitcase. She lay it down on the floor, ripped out the plastic security locks, unzipped it, and flipped open the top.

It all looked exactly as it had when she packed it. On top of it was the slip of paper with blue print that the airport security people always left.

She pulled her address book out of the side pocket and opened it. Right in the front cover, of course, was her name, address and phone number, in case she ever lost it.

And Richard and Natalie's address and phone number were in it, too.

"Time for a family meeting," she said.

Natalie stood next to her, chewing on a cuticle. Richard was on the telephone.

"Who's Richard talking to?" Sweetann asked.

Natalie shrugged.

"We're in too deep already," Sweetann said. She wished Natalie were huggable; she could use a hug. But she and Natalie had never even touched that Sweetann could remember. Natalie just remained distant. Sweetann had tried to make Natalie a sister, but there was some type of invisible barrier to closeness that surrounded Natalie. She stayed aloof, like she thought of herself as an exhibit. Natalie was to be admired but never touched.

They sat on the couch, looking at Sweetann's cheap clothes, waiting for Richard.

Sweetann stuck out a toe and flipped the top closed. She didn't want Natalie to look at her threadbare underwear.

Eventually, Richard came around the corner smiling.

"Lorenzo's coming over," he announced as if that were something that would make everybody smile.

The news tugged on Sweetann's heart in a conflicting way. She was hoping to see Lorenzo while here, hoping for a little romance in fact, but Richard must be insane to bring Lorenzo into this. On the other hand, maybe something like this could bind them together, make Lorenzo notice her.

Really notice her.

"Oh, Richard," Natalie said with disappointment in her voice. "Why Lorenzo?"

Sweetann looked at Natalie in surprise. She always thought Natalie liked Lorenzo, but dismay was clearly written on Natalie's face.

"Because he's a sleazebag, honey," Richard said, "and he can help us. Trust me on this one. Lorenzo is *exactly* what we need here."

Sweetann's face flushed. She had been attracted to Lorenzo from the first moment she met him several years ago at one of Richard and Natalie's famous barbecues. Now how could she pursue him, knowing how Richard and Natalie felt about him?

Worse yet, how could she be attracted to a sleazebag?

*Was Lorenzo a sleazebag?*

She had never thought so.

"You should have conferred with us before bringing someone else in on this," Natalie said. "That's another division of the... the...."

"I have a feeling there will be plenty to go around," Richard said.

"Sit down, Richard," Sweetann said. "We've got trouble already. Lorenzo is the least of our worries."

She brought them up to speed on the "William" who had called the house. She searched their faces for the expected look of horror that Nicky might be in danger. Sweetann wanted Richard to call a halt to the entire process before it went one second further in order to protect the young and innocent.

"Nobody is going to hurt Nick," Natalie said as if she were an authority about these things, her voice calm and cool as usual. Sweetann always thought of Natalie as beige. Beige hair, beige house, beige husband, beige voice. She even wore beige perfume. The house reeked of it, a perfume with no real scent. "They don't want him. If this William person wants the suitcase, he wants the suitcase. Not a little boy." Not even a flicker of a concern for Sweetann's son. "It was probably someone from work, just like he said."

What did Natalie know about what airport criminals did or did not want?

Natalie and Richard had no parental instincts at all. Giving them a baby would be the worst possible sentence for any child.

"Really, Sweetann," Richard said. "TSA goes through everybody's baggage. That doesn't mean anything. And isn't there somebody you work with named William? Bill? Will? Willie?"

*Bill Porter,* Sweetann remembered with a pinprick of hope. *Bill Porter said he wanted to come by and see Nicky's old bedroom furniture. Nicky was ready for something a little more sophisticated than a race car bed.*

"Regardless," Sweetann said, daring to feel a little better. "We've got to be smart, and we've got to be fast. They could be watching us already, so we've got to act as if everything is as normal and ordinary as possible. We've got to take care of business—*everything*—by the time my flight leaves on Sunday afternoon."

"Lorenzo is the key," Richard said. "We can be normal, and Lorenzo can be off-the-wall, as always. He's the one who will have to do all the dirty work. I don't know how to do that stuff."

Natalie nodded. She looked at Sweetann and nodded again. Sweetann nodded back, staring at Natalie. Sweetann wanted her share, she wanted it bad, but she felt her heart hardening against her brother and his wife. She would never forgive either one of them for not once even suggesting that Nicky's safety was more important than the contents of that suitcase.

They'd see this thing through, as insane as it suddenly was, and then Sweetann would have her say. Now that their parents were dead, perhaps there would be no further reason to keep in touch.

Richard gave Natalie a little nudge. "Make a pot of coffee, hon," he said.

Sweetann looked up the stairs toward the open bedroom door. Her attention was drawn there as if that suitcase had its own gravitational system.

She and Natalie stood up at the same time. "I'm going to go upstairs," Sweetann said.

Natalie walked around the coffee table, giving Richard a look Sweetann wished she hadn't seen. Richard stood, too. "I'll go with you," he said.

Fury building, Sweetann led her chaperone up the stairs.

The suitcase was exactly as they had left it. Richard opened it. Everything was undisturbed.

"We're going to have to trust each other," Sweetann said.

Richard flushed as if caught red-handed. Blushing was a family trait, but Richard had the corner on spinelessness. "Of course," he said, and Sweetann knew it wasn't Richard who didn't trust. Richard was fairly trustworthy, but Sweetann had known since the first moment she'd met Natalie that Natalie was not to be trusted at all.

And those who cannot be trusted do not trust others.

As if Richard had learned how to make it all better, he held out his arms and Sweetann accepted his hug. Natalie was not Richard's fault. He did well, just keeping his marriage together. That was more than Sweetann had managed to do.

While Richard zipped the suitcase, Sweetann pulled the shades. They had just started down the stairs together when they heard Lorenzo's Harley rumble up the drive.

Sweetann's heart beat faster and she ducked into the bathroom to check her teeth and face.

Her honey-colored hair showed a couple of wiry gray hairs in the part. It was cut in a bobbed style that for some reason seemed too young. She had nice light blue eyes, and at thirty-one, the tiny wrinkles around them weren't too deep or prominent. Her body was nothing special—she didn't have the tall, lean statuesque bearing that Natalie had, but she wasn't fat, either. Just kind of average. Average. A little bottom heavy, but mostly just average. That pretty much typified her, her life, her lifestyle, her aspirations...there were worse things than being average.

She dampened a towel and ran it under her eyes to catch

the smudges of mascara that had collected there over the past fourteen or so hours, fluffed her hair, and checked her teeth. She used some of the mouthwash that was in the medicine cabinet, gargled, and spit as she heard Lorenzo's deep voice in the kitchen.

*So what if he's a scumbag? You're not going to marry the guy,* she told herself in the mirror. *And who gives a shit what Natalie thinks, anyway?*

Four years ago, when Lorenzo showed up unannounced and apparently uninvited at Richard and Natalie's barbecue, he had long black hair, a full beard, and wore dirty Levis and a ragged blue jean jacket. He had nervous eyes, and wanted to talk privately with Richard.

A glimpse was all Sweetann got of him, but there was something about him, something about those bright, intense blue eyes amidst all that black hair that struck a chord.

The next year, she and Nicky came down again, and Lorenzo stopped by minus the beard. His jeans were clean, and he wore a long-sleeved shirt. The haunted nervousness in his eyes had disappeared.

When he showed up unannounced at her annual trip two years ago, she began to believe that he was keeping track of her visits. He seemed genuinely happy to see her, paid a nominal amount of attention to Nicky, and they verged on some light flirting.

Then last year, the flirting was full-bore. Whatever changes Lorenzo was making in his life shone through those piercing blue eyes that gave her chills whenever they looked directly into hers. And he had that shy smile. He came into the house, sat down next to her, put his arm around the back of the sofa, and before she knew it, he was playing with her hair.

That was the type of thing that got the attention of a celibate, divorced thirty-one-year-old with a kid.

She hadn't stopped thinking of him since.

She adjusted her pink cotton sweater and jeans, spritzed on some perfume that she found in the cabinet under the sink, pronounced herself presentable, and went to meet the man who had occupied her idle thoughts since the last time she had come to LA.

She tried to bring Nicky with her every year, but this year, she and Richard had business to take care of with their parents' estate, and this was the only time she could get away. Nicky was in a school play and in the middle of rehearsals, so he couldn't leave. The only thing to do was to come to LA by herself and leave Nicky with Charlotte for the weekend.

She never thought that a weekend of great sex would be in her future, although the possibility had crossed her mind more than once, but now that she was here, and Lorenzo was here, she was kind of glad Nicky was back in Seattle.

Lorenzo leaned against the refrigerator, a Diet Coke in one hand, his long, leather-clad legs crossed at the ankle. His dark hair was cut short, something Sweetann didn't expect, but it looked good, and accentuated that amazing dark blue of his eyes. Freckles sprinkled across his nose, giving him a touch of the young innocent look, charmingly incongruous with his attire and his attitude.

"Sweets!" he said, and held out his arms.

"Hi, Lorenzo," she said, and melted into his lanky warmth. He squeezed her a little too tight a little too long, with Richard and Natalie's eyes on her back, but it felt good, so good she got a little dizzy. It had been a long time since she'd had such a suggestive hug.

She told him with body language during that long hug and shy grind that she could be available. He got the message.

"You're still adorable," he said. "Where's Nicky?"

"Home," she said, and tried to hide the grin that came along with that one word.

"Good," he whispered, and brushed his lips across her forehead.

Face hot and flushed, she pulled back and looked at the floor. She felt as though everybody was watching her as she got a coffee cup from the cabinet and poured herself a full one. "Coffee, anyone?" At Richard's nod, she poured one for him. Natalie poured herself a scotch, and looked Richard squarely and defiantly in the eyes as she took the first swallow.

"Let's go into the living room," Richard suggested, and moved in that direction. Natalie followed him, and Lorenzo waited for Sweetann to go next, and he put a hand on the small of her back as he followed.

It was a tiny gesture, but it ignited a flame with great potential.

Relax, Sweetann counseled herself. There are important things to do.

Natalie and Richard settled on the sofa, Lorenzo collapsed into the easy chair and motioned for Sweetann to sit on his lap. She touched him on the shoulder with a shy smile and said, "No, we've got some serious talking to do first."

He heard the "first" part and smiled. God, he was gorgeous, with those flashing white teeth.

And he knew it.

There was something about that dark hair and those dark blue eyes. Sweetann sat on a suede ottoman and put her coffee cup carefully on a marble coaster.

"So?" Lorenzo said, then swigged his soda. "What's up?"

"What have you been doing lately?" Richard asked.

A frown crossed lightly over Lorenzo's face. It seemed to Sweetann that Richard's question had turned this evening into a job interview. That was too many switches for her. An hour ago, it had been the beginning of a pleasant weekend with her brother and his wife, doing a little family business, signing some legal papers, maybe taking in a movie or seeing some local sights. Then the suitcase upstairs had brought intrigue and fear. Then Lorenzo showed up and brought in and some serious sexual interest. Now she was afraid she was about to smell the grilling of Lorenzo's flesh.

"This and that," he said warily. "You know. Paying the rent."

"You clean?"

Lorenzo calmly set his Coke can on a coaster, then unbuttoned his sleeves. With infuriating calmness, never taking his eyes off Richard's, he rolled his sleeves up and showed everyone the silver injection and abscess scars that ran up and down the inside of his forearms. Nothing fresh. "Six years clean and sober, Richard," he said. "I thought you knew that."

"We've got a situation," Sweetann said, wanting to diffuse the situation.

"An opportunity," Natalie said.

"We need you to be trustworthy and reliable," Richard said.

"Fine," Lorenzo said evenly and without malice as he buttoned his cuffs. "What's up?"

Sweetann stood. "I'll show you," she said, and held out her hand to him. She looked at Richard. "Time is of the essence, you guys. We don't know what they know."

Lorenzo took her hand and stood.

She looked up at him. "Bad guys."

Natalie and Richard sat on the couch frowning at the two of them. "Okay," Sweetann said. "Come on. Chaperone us."

Natalie jumped up, pulled Richard up, and the four filed up the stairs to open the suitcase yet one more time.

"Man oh man," Lorenzo breathed when Richard opened the suitcase. Instead of being afraid, or in awe, he reached right in and pulled out a rubber-banded pack of hundred dollar bills. "How many are here?"

"I don't know," Richard said. "None of us has touched them."

"Well, it won't bite," Lorenzo said, and handed the pack to him. He picked up two others and handed one to each of the women.

"How much?" Sweetann asked as she hefted the bundle.

Lorenzo buzzed the end. "My guess is that there's about a hundred bills to a pack." He stacked them on the bed and did a quick count. "Fifty packs. Jeez. How much is that?"

"Half a million," Richard said.

"But that's not the main attraction," Lorenzo said, and all eyes went back to the suitcase, to the six tan brick-sized packages, wrapped in clear plastic. "That's some serious dope. There's your *real* money, kids," Lorenzo said. He sat down on the bed. "Jesus Christ, I used to pray for a sight like that. And now it scares the bejesus out of me."

"What is it?" Sweetann asked.

"I don't know," Lorenzo said. "And I can't taste it to find out. Cocaine, I imagine. Or heroin. Some designer drug, maybe. I don't know. But I've been clean for six years, and I'm not about to jeopardize that."

"Can you sell it?" Natalie asked.

Lorenzo scoffed. "Sure. No problem with that. Except that I'd go to prison for the rest of my life."

"Let's divide the money and flush the drugs," Sweetann said. "A hundred thousand dollars for each of us is enough for one night's work."

"Let's go downstairs and talk about it," Natalie said. But nobody moved. They all just stood there, staring down at the contents of the open suitcase. Reluctantly, Richard flipped the suitcase closed and they all looked up at each other as if awakened.

"Powerful shit," Lorenzo said, putting words to the mesmerizing effect.

Richard zipped the suitcase and stood it back in the corner of the room, then they all filed back downstairs.

"Whoever lost this isn't going to care if he lost one brick or the whole fucking suitcase," Lorenzo said as they settled back in the living room. "He's going to want it back and he's going to want it back bad. If we're going to keep it, it's got to be worth our while. And there is definite risk. Oh yes, there is risk."

Sweetann saw how easily he threw that "we" into the conversation. "We're way over our heads here, guys," she said. "C'mon, let's take it back to the airport."

"No way," Natalie said.

Lorenzo grinned at her. "You have no idea what you're messing with here, Natalie."

"Well," Richard said. "What do we do now?"

Lorenzo smiled, a wicked smile, a smile that made Sweetann's parts hum. "I could use a cup of that coffee," he said.

# Chapter 2

Natalie looked at that suitcase full of cash and thought, "There's our baby."

Richard made what he considered a good living as a software engineer, but there was never enough. And now this fertility thing. Natalie needed an extra fifty thousand dollars or so, just to make sure they could keep at the in vitro until it took. But they were out of cash.

In vitro was expensive. Out went the cash and in came the debt.

Richard had said *no more,* but he wasn't a woman. He didn't know what baby hunger was like. He didn't know what it meant to see that blood stain on her panties every month. He didn't know what it meant to be barren. It was her fault, not his. He had no idea what she went through.

Getting pregnant and carrying a baby had been so effortless for Sweetann… It wasn't fair. That was something that Natalie had in mind to talk to Sweetann about this weekend. Maybe Sweetann would do her big brother a favor and carry a baby in her overly-fertile womb for them. Free.

But with this cash, Natalie didn't have to ask. She could buy her own baby, and seal Richard to her forever.

Maybe then they could act like a family.

She looked up at Lorenzo and wished, for the millionth time, that the sterility problem were on Richard's side. She'd hustle Lorenzo into her bed in an instant. And boom. Baby on board.

Natalie squirmed on the sofa thinking about Lorenzo naked, his long, lean form stretched out next to her. Then Richard put his hand protectively on her shoulder and she tried to stay with the pace of the conversation.

Lorenzo and Sweetann seemed to be masterminding this operation. All she had to do was keep prodding them onward and protect her interests.

She looked at Lorenzo, sprawled in a wing chair, coffee cup balanced easily on one black-leathered knee. Lorenzo and

Richard had been unlikely comrades from their college days, but Richard had straightened up, got his degree, married Natalie and become respectable. Lorenzo had gone from beer to pot to shooting smack and it took an overdose and a lengthy rehabilitation to turn him around.

When he got clean, he had looked Richard up, much to Natalie's disgust, and Richard had helped him out. For a while, Lorenzo had been Richard's charity case, and Natalie allowed it. But against all odds, Lorenzo had proved himself, and now stood on his own. He'd gotten a little education and worked as a draftsman in an architectural firm. He wanted to be a landscape architect.

This money would pay for lots of classes. Natalie could buy her baby, Lorenzo could buy his degree, Sweetann could buy herself some new clothes—Lord knew she needed some, and Richard could buy—what would Richard buy?

Some bauble for his stupid fucking mistress, probably.

Natalie gritted her teeth and pushed the thought away.

It hadn't taken long before Lorenzo became quite good fantasy material for Natalie's fertile imagination. Richard felt he was doing something positive by giving a helping hand to an old friend who was trying so desperately to climb out of the gutter, and Natalie stood by on the sidelines and watched Lorenzo move, his teeth white, his eyes deep blue, his long black hair shaggy, shiny and curly, his large hands clean, his nails manicured.

And to Natalie's amazement, they both began to admire Lorenzo, although she would never admit it out loud. Lorenzo was the bad boy, doing all the outrageous things Richard had always been too conservative to do. They were polar opposites, and they enjoyed each other's company. Calling him in on this deal was a natural for Richard.

She watched Lorenzo and Sweetann talk to each other for a minute. She could feel the magnetism between them all the way on the other side of the living room. It warmed the room, and ignited a bit of Natalie's jealous streak.

She looked over at Richard, and tried to send him a psychic message: *If we could get Sweetann to throw away her diaphragm tonight, we just might get ourselves a baby. The natural way. The*

27

*easy way. The cheap way. And have lots of money to spend on baby clothes, instead of giving it all to the fertility clinic.*

Richard rubbed Natalie's shoulder, giving no indication that he received her message. She sucked down the scotch and pretended to be intent on what Lorenzo was saying.

"Sunday afternoon? You're out of your fuckin' mind," Lorenzo said to Sweetann. He crossed his legs and turned away from her.

"Listen to me," Sweetann said. She leaned forward from her perch on the ottoman, put a hand on his arm and pulled him back toward her. "We have to act as if everything is normal. I can't be changing my plans, I can't change my ticket. We have to act as if everything is absolutely the same as always. We turn the lights out when it's bedtime, even if we stay up all night. Natalie and I will go shopping tomorrow, because that's what we do. Natalie will buy clothes, I'll buy something for Nick, we'll have salads for lunch. Richard will play golf. You need to sell that stuff. Tomorrow."

"Okay," Lorenzo said. "I've heard your little fantasy. Now you listen to me."

"Wait," Sweetann said, smiling, and Natalie could see how much she was enjoying the tension of their dialogue. These two were made for each other.

Natalie wondered if she and Richard had ever had that kind of attraction for each other. If Lorenzo could stay clean, Sweetann would make him a hell of a wife.

"I'm not finished yet," Sweetann said. "These bad guys, there's the tiniest possibility that they opened my suitcase, looked in my address book and might know where Nicky is, they might know where we are. I don't believe that's true, not for a second, or I'd never go along with this, but there is that possibility. You need to really get that, Lorenzo. We're talking about a whole lot of money up there, and I don't want to risk my neck, or Nicky's, by stretching this thing out. I want to go in fast and do the deal and be done with it. Then I want to get the hell out of town. With my kid. Safe."

Silence.

"And I won't leave this house without my share," she added, then looked down at her fingers.

Natalie stiffened, taking that as a personal insult. She kept her silence.

"Are you finished?" Lorenzo asked. "May I speak now, please?"

Sweetann looked up at him, nodded, then looked back at her fingertips.

"Okay," Lorenzo said. "I agree with all that, looking normal and all. The truth is, anybody could have picked up that suitcase. Somebody at the airport fucked up by putting it on the carousel. Chances are, they have no idea who has it, so I'd stop worrying about your boy. But if you don't give me room to move, time to negotiate, then you drastically reduce the value of the merchandise. If they think we're up against a wall, they'll take advantage of it."

"That's why I called you," Richard said. "If anybody can pull it off, you can. You don't have to let on what wall we're up against. You can tell them you have another offer that expires at noon on Sunday or whatever.... I have confidence in you, Lorenzo. For a quarter share of what's upstairs, I believe you can pull it off."

"Excuse me?" Natalie said, heat flushing through her for the second time in less than two minutes. She stared daggers into Richard. "One quarter?"

"Hey," Lorenzo said. "You're shopping, he's playing golf, I'm doing the work. Fuck yes, a quarter share. At *least* a quarter share."

He finished his coffee, then set the cup down right next to the coaster. "Just who the fuck do you think would be going to prison for fucking ever if I got busted? You?" Then he reached over and grabbed Sweetann's hand. "Half," he said, just for the added effect, "for me and the sweet one here."

Sweetann looked like she was in heaven.

Aggravation and jealousy hit Natalie like a two by four between the eyes. She gripped her Scotch glass with one hand and Richard's knee with the other.

"It's fair," Richard said, moving Natalie's talons from his leg. He set his coffee cup on a coaster and leaned forward, putting his elbows on his knees. "Okay, so what's the plan?"

"First thing," Sweetann said, "is that no one else knows. *No one*, Richard."

Richard sat back as if he had been slapped. "Hey, I just called Lorenzo, and it was a good call."

"It was," Sweetann admitted, "but you should have okayed it with us first. Nobody else. *Nobody.*" She looked at Natalie, who nodded. She looked at Lorenzo, who agreed.

"Okay, Lorenzo," she said, "do you know how to go about selling it?"

"I have a couple of ideas," he said. "I'd like to take a taste into town tonight and see what kind of interest I can scrape up."

"Tonight?"

He gave her an affectionate smile and squeezed her hand. "You want this thing done by Sunday noon, I say it will be."

Sweetann smiled at Lorenzo, smiled at Richard, smiled at Natalie, and Natalie, though scowling, knew this was about getting rich. She could put up with anything, even this bullshit, for that kind of money upstairs. Richard had done exactly the right thing by inviting Lorenzo into the deal.

And when it came to dividing up the cash evenly at the end of the deal—well, that remained to be seen. She wasn't certain it was going to be divided into quarters.

Within another half hour, Lorenzo and Sweetann had gone, a handful of little folded papers, each with a dollop of tan powder inside, tucked inside Lorenzo's wallet. They had taken Richard's BMW, against Natalie's better judgment, and left Richard and Natalie home alone with a suitcase full of money and drugs.

It made Natalie feel curiously invincible. With half a million dollars, they could just jump on a plane and be gone.

Right now. Right this minute.

But a half million wouldn't last them long enough. There was more to be had. She'd wait.

That they might need to elude bad guys forever was a vaguely uncomfortable thought that Natalie preferred not to consider.

Richard wrapped his arms around her as they stood by the kitchen door listening to Sweetann and Lorenzo pull out of the garage. He still had the two brand new hundred-dollar bills in his hand, she could hear them crinkle in his fist as she hugged him back. Her two were in her pocket.

That was a stroke of genius, she thought, her suggestion that they each slip two hundred-dollar bills out of a packet. Sweetann and Lorenzo might need them tonight, and just doing it gave everybody a power surge. Another carrot that Natalie dangled to induce everybody to do her bidding.

Masterful, if she did say so herself.

"Let's go look at it again," she whispered.

"No," he said. "We agreed not to."

"I know," she said, looking up at him with her best coy look, "but let's be naughty."

Richard sighed and nodded in resignation.

He followed her upstairs. Natalie pulled the bills from her pocket and rubbed them on her cheek, breathing in the inky smell.

Richard opened the guest room closet and pulled out the suitcase, put it on the bed, unzipped the top, and flipped it open.

It looked exactly the same. Nobody would know that eight hundred-dollar bills were missing, and nobody would even notice the piece of scotch tape over the small slice in one brick. Lorenzo had torn a page out of Natalie's Victoria's Secret catalog, had Sweetann tear it into three-inch squares, while he slit open the brick with his penknife. Then he folded four of those squares into origami-like envelopes, lifted powder out on his little knife blade, filled the envelopes, refolded them and put them in his wallet. He wouldn't touch it, or smell it or anything. Good. One good snort of that stuff and Lorenzo might just as well put a gun to his head.

Or so he said.

Then he'd taped over the little slice, and the two of them took off.

Natalie reached over and picked at the edge of the tape with a long, tapered fingernail.

"What are you doing?"

"I'm curious," she said.

"Please don't," Richard said.

"I'm not going to hurt anything," she said. She got the

plate of potpourri from the nightstand and dumped the flower petals into the trash can, then with the corner of one of her hundred-dollar bills, shoveled a little of the powder out of the brick and onto the plate.

"You must have snorted a little coke in college," she said.

"That was a long time ago," Richard said. "And we don't know that this is coke."

"Of course it is," she said, then pulled out a little more, and a little more after that for good measure. "What else could it be?" Then she pressed the tape back down.

The expression on Richard's face told her he didn't like this. He didn't like the fact that she wasn't going to her AA meetings any more, he didn't like the fact that she was drinking again, although he had admitted she had it pretty well under control, but he clearly didn't like the idea of her snorting some cocaine. But he went along with it anyway. She knew he would. He was intrigued.

"Remember how erotic cocaine is?" She teased him with a brazen smile and a cocked eyebrow, then swirled out of the room.

A moment later, he joined her on their bed, as she sat cross legged, rolling up one of the hundred dollar bills.

"Ready?" She felt an excitement she hadn't felt since those cocaine-fueled college days. She felt sexy and naughty and ready for a good romp, even if it was only with her husband. She tried not to think that it had been watching Lorenzo and Sweetann that had started her juices flowing.

She tried not to think that she and Richard hadn't had satisfactory sex since they started trying to conceive years ago. What they had now was utilitarian sex. Maybe all that was about to change. She was horny and it was borne of jealousy and the promise of some good dope. Richard gave her a long kiss full of excitement and promise.

"Ready," he said.

She put rolled bill to her nose and began to vacuum up the powder.

# Chapter 3

Nicky sprawled on the couch, the script with his lines highlighted in yellow drooping from his slack fingers.

Something weird was going on with his mom.

He replayed their phone conversation again in his mind, but there weren't enough clues for him to figure out exactly what she was thinking.

"Charlotte?"

"Hmmm?" Charlotte was sitting in his mom's chair, painting her fingernails dark red and watching a Buffy rerun.

"What did Mom say to you when she called?"

"Nothing," Charlotte said. "Just what to do if there's an emergency."

"Emergency," Nicky repeated quietly. That wasn't a good sign. "What are we supposed to do if there's an emergency?"

"Call my mom," Charlotte said. "Shush now, this is the good part." Charlotte capped her polish and blew on her fingertips, her attention riveted to the television.

Nicky waved away the stink of the polish with the pages of his script. He ought to be studying, but instead, he had a creepy feeling.

Any kind of an emergency he could think of, he'd call 911, not Charlotte's mom.

The apartment never felt right with his mom gone. More than empty, the whole place seemed unimportant, even his room with all his cool stuff. And that was bad enough for a whole weekend with play tryouts, without strange things happening. Like that William guy calling, and his mom calling right afterward, talking about emergency procedures.

Nick sat up and looked at Charlotte.

Maybe they ought to go over to her mom's house now. Maybe he ought to suggest it, since Charlotte wouldn't. She liked coming over and pretending she was a grownup.

"Did she say what kind of an emergency?" Nick asked.

"Shush," Charlotte said, her attention on the television. "Get ready for bed." She started shaking the nail polish bottle again, and Nick knew she was about to torture her toes with that awful color.

He got up and went to his bedroom to change into his pajamas. The sooner he went to sleep, the sooner the weekend would pass and his mom would come home. There wouldn't be any emergencies when she was around. There never were.

He hoped there wouldn't be any emergencies when she was gone.

He brushed his teeth and jumped into bed with his script, but had trouble concentrating on it. The word EMERGENCY kept flashing off and on in his mind like a sign he'd seen once driving by the hospital.

He whispered his way through the play, working each line as the director had suggested, hoping that somehow he'd magically memorize them while sleeping. Eventually, he turned off his reading light and stared through the dark at the Superman poster on his wall. The Man of Steel was illuminated by a tiny nightlight by the door.

Nick closed his eyes and listened to the television in the living room. Buffy was gone, and now she was watching an old rerun of 90210.

Charlotte was all right, but she had never been his favorite. He had a feeling she was the ugly nerd in high school, but barely smart enough to be really nerdy. She tried too hard to show him how cool she was, but really, what did she care what he thought? She was in high school and he was still in grade school.

And yet, he hoped he'd be smart enough to handle any crisis that came up, because he had a feeling that when it came to an emergency situation, he'd be the adult in charge, not Charlotte.

# Chapter 4

Lorenzo had been born under a lucky star, or so his Italian grandmother had told him, and he had always counted on that to see him through. So far, so good. But this score, this big score, as irresistible as it was, might be pushing his luck a little too seriously.

Back in the old days, he would have looked at that amount of smack or coke or whatever the hell it was, and he would have done whatever it took to gain possession of it.

Then he would hoard it. A lifetime supply—for a very short lifetime.

A lifetime supply of death, because sure as shit, he would have overdosed. Either that, or he would have gotten himself killed over it for being too careless. Or got himself stoned and stupid and ripped off.

But like all losers, he dreamed of the big score. He always felt he was destined for great things, and the fact that he was not in prison, but clean and sober instead, just seemed to confirm that.

So this suitcase: was it his Big Chance that would set him up for life, or was it the Big Temptation that was going to send him straight to hell?

He'd rather die than put that shit in his nose or in a vein. That was the one thing about which he was absolutely certain.

"I love this car," he said to Sweetann as he took a corner a little faster than he normally would. "It's like a little Sherman tank with zip." He felt a little reckless and that was not a good sign. He was high, just having the drugs in his wallet, nestled up against his butt.

Or maybe it was having Sweetann in the seat next to him.

He wasn't sure. Whatever it was, it felt dangerous. It had been too long since he had felt dangerous.

An hour ago, feeling dangerous was not a good thing. Right now, though, it was a great thing.

"Lorenzo," Sweetann said in her soft voice. She put a tiny hand on his arm. "Want to pull over and talk about this for a minute?"

Yes, he did. Yes indeedy he did.

"Nothing to talk about," he said.

"Please?"

With a sigh, Lorenzo pulled into a Safeway parking lot, backed into a parking space as far from the store as he could get, turned off the ignition and lights, then pushed the seat back and looked at her. That damned stuff in his wallet was burning a hole in his butt.

"I have a few friends in AA," Sweetann said, "and so I can imagine how much your sobriety means."

Lorenzo smoothed a rough, worn patch on the knee of his leather pants with his thumb.

This wasn't the Big Chance, he decided. This was the Big Temptation.

Did he want to go to hell? Did he want to go to jail? Did he want to live a life worse than death?

"I just want to make sure you're up for this," she said. "There's no reason you have to go through any of it."

"Are you having second thoughts?" Lorenzo asked.

"Yeah, sure. Of course. I have a lot at stake if things go wrong. You've met Nicky, but I'd like you to have the chance to really get to know him. And that won't happen if we're dead, or if you're dead or in jail. Of course I'm having second thoughts."

"Why didn't you speak up?"

"Natalie has a way of...I don't know."

"Manipulating."

"Yeah."

"Yeah, well," Lorenzo said, "I'm willing to take this another step and see what happens. We can always bail. We can always return the suitcase or dump it in the river."

"So the selling drugs part, it doesn't interfere with your spiritual program?"

Lorenzo didn't want to hear that. "If it isn't me, it's somebody else," he said, and turned the key in the ignition.

That was a stupid fucking thing to say, and the weakest of the rationalizations and justifications he could come up with. He didn't know why he said that, and was sorry he had.

He didn't want to talk about this, he just wanted to do it.

He didn't want to examine himself too closely. If he did, he'd bail right now. He could give lip service to that "if I don't sell dope to kids, somebody else will," bullshit all night long, but it wasn't going to change the fact that it did indeed interfere with his spiritual program. Rigorous honesty, the Big Book said.

And once he began to lie to himself, and to others, then his sobriety was in serious jeopardy.

"Lorenzo?"

He turned and looked at her and she looked like a fucking goddess in this hazy light. She had that classic All-American girl-next-door look. Not sleazy and overdone, not young and innocent, just clean. Blonde. Freckled. He liked it.

From the first moment he saw her in Richard's back yard, he hoped that some day he'd be worthy of someone like Sweetann.

She had just picked a toasted hot dog bun off the barbecue and put it on a plate for a little boy. They were having a discussion about condiments.

Lorenzo was jangling from a run-in with some old drugging buddies. They had just scored, and the skag in that little bag began to sweet talk Lorenzo from ten feet away. *Just a little taste,* it said. *C'mon, Lorenzo, don't you remember what a good time we used to have together?* He hadn't even been clean for two years yet, and sometimes life was hard. He knew the answer to going through a difficult time was not more smack, but boy, he knew it would erase all the pain he was going through trying to sweep out the detritus of his past and live the clean and sober lifestyle.

He hadn't seen any of his old friends since he got clean, and the ease with which he related to those two sick junkies and fell right in with their excitement over a fresh score scared him.

It also made him want to go with them.

He fell easily in beside them as they began walking, looking for an alley, or a doorway, a toilet, or a bush to hide behind, so they could boil that crap up in a spoon over a Bic and slide it, still steaming hot, into his greedy veins. He walked with them, his old druggie pals, his mind desperately seeking a way out while his body followed along like a well-trained dog.

The next NA meeting wasn't for two hours. The next AA meeting wasn't until much later. He had a wallet full of phone numbers, and the AA seventh step prayer on a little card, but he had no phone, and a prayer seemed like pretty flimsy stuff when compared to the overpowering temptation of that little bag of heroin.

Where could he go?

Jack's house was too far away.

*Richard.*

Freedom flushed through him. "Just remembered something," he said to his junkie acquaintances, and spun around. "Gotta go."

Those fucking smackheads didn't even notice. They had their own priorities.

Lorenzo went directly to Richard's house, rattled by the close call, hoping to hang out for a couple of hours until the meeting. He was surprised to find a big party going on in Richard's back yard, a party to which he had not been invited, nor was he particularly welcome.

He didn't care. He desperately needed normalcy.

And he saw it. He saw a short blonde with blue eyes, a hot dog bun and a little boy, and something turned over inside him.

*Someday,* he thought. *Someday, I'll deserve something like that.*

And here she was. He'd worked hard to make himself worthy, even keeping loosely in touch with Richard and popping in on his sister's annual visits. Sweetann Holt. Everything he thought he wanted in a woman.

Except for that name. What was with that name?

She reached a little hand up and touched his cheek and he wanted to check in to the nearest motel and spend all night in there with this adorable girl, come home in the morning, clean, sober, with a fresh-faced giggly girl on his arm and tell Natalie to shove her money and her dope up her well-oiled, well-groomed and refined little twat.

Sweetann leaned into him, kissed him on the corner of his mouth. She smelled like some spice, and her lips were so soft he felt he could bed down right there for the night. He put a hand around the back of her head and brought her lips squarely onto his and gave her a long, soft kiss that stirred him almost as much as the sight of all that money and all that powder.

He wanted out, he wanted out of this stupid deal real bad. He wanted to be squeaky clean, go back to a Narcotics Anonymous meeting and confess his triumph over temptation so severe that he almost sold his soul.

Instead, he was going to flirt with selling his soul, his sobriety, and perhaps the lives of this fine woman and her son. He was going to descend into the gritty scum pits where the waters were most foul, and he was going to take a little swim.

He knew it and he was helpless to stop himself.

He might drown.

And Sweetann was right by his side.

"I think I should take you back to Richard's," he said, his lips against her soft cheek.

"No way," she said. "I'm with you on this. We'll keep each other out of trouble."

He pulled back and looked into her innocent, trusting eyes.

She had no idea about the scum they would have to deal with. He shook his head. They were doomed, and she had no idea.

He turned on the headlights, put Richard's BMW into gear and, in silence, headed downtown.

Ten quiet minutes later, he pulled into a weedy parking lot and came to a stop next to a vandalized Pontiac. The brick building had no face on this side, only a metal door and a dumpster in the corner.

"What is this place?" Sweetann asked.

"An old hangout. Why don't you stay here?"

"No way," she said, looking around with wide eyes.

She's right, he thought. She'll be safer inside. "C'mon, then." He locked the car and she took his hand and they walked across the pitched and cracked sidewalk around the building to the front. Not much of a face there, either. A neon beer sign in one dark window. No welcome mat.

Lorenzo opened the door and they walked into a stinking dingy tavern, where two guys played pool in the far corner, one drunk slept with his head on the bar, and a lone stream of cigarette smoke, like an antenna, rose from the corner booth.

"Sit at the bar," Lorenzo told her, and he stood with her

while she hiked up onto a barstool. The bartender came over, laid a napkin in front of her.

"Diet Coke," she said.

"Same," Lorenzo said, and when it came, he sipped it, leaning against the bar, looking around.

Pool balls cracked against each other, the bartender's television had the late news on low volume, the drunk twitched and muttered, and the antenna of smoke never wavered.

"Be right back," he said to Sweetann, heart hammering because he belonged in sleazy places like this. He used to fucking *live* in places like this, and he didn't want to any more. Please God, don't make me sink back down to this level again.

He pushed off from the bar and walked toward the corner booth.

"Hello, Charles," Lorenzo said as he slid along the red vinyl bench seat on the opposite side of the table.

The old man looked up expressionless, then after a moment, his rheumy eyes gained recognition and his pale, spotted face broke into a genuine grin. "Lorenzo, my boy. Look at you!"

Lorenzo relaxed a smidgen. Charles was glad to see him. Or maybe Charles was just happy to have a little company.

Charles had aged terribly in the six years since Lorenzo had seen him. Maybe it was the smoking. Maybe it was sitting in this dim place night after night after night. Pushing seventy, an old dope runner, this was his semi-retirement, still in middle management. More than most dope runners could hope for. Charles was still here because while he sold drugs, he never took them. His forehead was mottled with liver spots and his eyes, behind trifocals, were red-rimmed and watery. His teeth were newly store bought and too white.

Charles slid a torn off matchbook top to mark his place in the paperback he'd been reading and set it aside. The cigarette smoldering in the ashtray died. Charles lit another, took a deep drag, then set it in the ashtray to burn down in a long ash, its plume of smoke rising straight to the stained acoustic ceiling. "We haven't seen you lately."

"No, I've been on to other things."

"So I see. So I see. You look well."

Lorenzo nodded in acknowledgement. He wished he could

return the compliment.

"What brings you here tonight?" Charles asked.

Lorenzo pulled out his wallet, selected a paper envelope and put it on the table, trying not to look around nervously. His feet were moving restlessly, his elbows were on the table, he was leaning too close to Charles, too close to Charles's cigarette.

With a deep breath, he pulled back, stilled his muscles, calmed his face and waited to see what Charles had to say.

With soft, gentle hands, Charles opened the envelope and looked inside. He smelled it, then he wet his pinky finger, dabbed it into the powder and put the taste to his tongue.

"You have a quantity?"

Lorenzo nodded.

"A kilo?"

Lorenzo nodded.

"More?"

Lorenzo nodded again, not exactly sure how much he should divulge.

Charles licked his lips, refolded the paper and put it in his shirt pocket. "Tastes a little bit like..." Charles feigned a fuzzy memory, then zeroed in on Lorenzo's eyes, "a little bit like airport smack," he said.

Lorenzo's face flushed. "Does it?"

"That heroin's hot shit, Lorenzo. Are you up to the task?"

"I don't know, Charles, am I?"

Now it was Charles's turn to move in closer, speak in a low, conspiratorial tone. "I'm not going to waste your time, Lorenzo. If I do that, I increase your chances of losing. I won't stand in your way of a big score; I'd never do that. Those airport thugs are no friends of mine. I'd love to see you profit from their stupidity. Spike is at the zoo. If I were you, I'd have it done before dawn."

Lorenzo nodded, slid out from the booth. He held his hand out for Charles to shake. "It's good to see you again, my friend."

Charles took his hand and looked at Lorenzo with what seemed like affection. Lorenzo had never seen that quality of Charles before, but then Lorenzo had always been smacked out whenever he met Charles, and there was no reason in the world Charles would have respected him then. Now, Lorenzo was clean and he looked good. Charles had to respect that. Lorenzo did.

They shook hands and parted, Lorenzo smiling at the sight of Sweetann sitting at the bar, waiting for him.

"What time is it?" he asked her as they whisked out the door.

"Eleven-fifty," she said, consulting the face of her cell phone. "How'd it go?"

"There was good news and there was bad news," Lorenzo said. "The good news was that I haven't burned any of those bridges. The bad news is that Charles knew it was from the airport."

"What do you mean?" Sweetann grabbed his arm, but that didn't slow down his pace. She trotted to keep up with him. "What do you mean he knew it was from the airport? Are you kidding me? Oh, my god."

"Yeah."

"Holy smoke," she said, slowing her pace. "We're already in pretty deep, aren't we?"

"Yeah. News travels fast."

Lorenzo beeped the car unlocked, they both got in, Lorenzo put the key in the ignition and then stopped. "We've gone about as far as we can and still turn around," he said, thinking first of Charles, and then of the legendary airport guys, then of Spike and his no-conscience, pain-for-pleasure, wretchedly dangerous, scummy gang. He thought not only of his own hide, but of Sweetann's little boy.

Sweetann looked up at him, her trusting eyes glinting in the pale streetlights.

"I had hoped to just unload it on Charles, but he wasn't taking it. I'll tell you when we pass the point of no return, and it's not far from here. But right now, we can still back out."

"What do you think?" she asked.

"Hell, Sweets," Lorenzo said, fiddling with the keys. "A big score is every drug addict's dream. I can't tell you how many hours I've spent talking, dreaming, scheming about it." He looked over at her, ran his hand over her silky hair. "But I'm just a small time loser, honey, and you've got a kid. The stakes are far higher for you."

"What are our chances, do you think?"

Lorenzo shrugged. "They're not nice men, and they don't play fair. If we pull this off, catching your plane home on Sunday isn't going to be an issue. It isn't even going to be possible. They'll know we're in on it, so we'll be on the run as soon as we get cash in hand. So will Natalie and Richard."

"And Nick."

"And Nick. You be thinking about this, Sweets. You be thinking, I be driving." He leaned over for a whiff of that delicious scent, kissed her tremendously kissable lips, lingered there longer than he should have, waiting, hoping that Sweetann would grab a fistful of his shirt front and suck his bottom lip. Then they could tumble into the back seat and forget all about Charles and Spike and the rest of it.

She was an oasis, this girl.

But she didn't start them down that preferred road, so he reluctantly centered himself back into driving mode and eased the car out of the parking lot.

# Chapter 5

The powder was like no cocaine Natalie had ever seen. It was tan, not white, and it didn't sparkle quite like the coke she used to snort in college. As soon as it was in her nose, she knew it wasn't coke at all. She didn't know what it was, but she was afraid she'd already tooted too much of it.

It burned differently. It burned like a metal brush in her nostril. It tasted bad, too, in the back of her throat. This wasn't the bitter tang of cocaine, but had a bad, dead taste, like old leaves.

She was hoping to get a good buzz, maybe do some kinky sex with Richard, maybe get a little jacked up and go dancing or something.

But that wasn't happening. Not at all. Sex, or dancing, or anything but just lying still was absolutely out of the question.

She lay back on the pillows, and felt Richard take the tubed bill from her hand. She heard him begin to snort the powder in the bowl and she barely got a warning out, "Be careful," she said, or she thought she said, at least she wanted to say, and then she didn't much care any more. Her muscles didn't want to move. Her eyes didn't want to open, her mouth didn't want to work.

Which was fine.

Richard could take care of himself.

Natalie felt a flush of panic when the feeling came on so hard, so fast, but a second later, she forgot to be afraid in the extraordinary surge of calm. Tensions melted, worries evaporated. She didn't care about being barren, she didn't mind that she had married a loser who was most assuredly cheating on her, she forgot about the fact that gravity was doing terrible things to her face. What mattered was that she could feel this peace, this soft, wonderful, floating pleasure.

It was incredible.

First her feet went away, then her lower legs. She could move them, at least she was sure she could if she wanted to, but she didn't want to. Then the feeling in her hands went, and her arms, and she lay gently, lightly on the bed, a torso, and then only a face, feeling light and leaden at the same time, weightless and yet one with the bed. She felt Richard lie down next to her, heard him say something, but she wasn't interested. She felt wonderful. Total calm. Total control. Or total lack of control. Maybe that was it. Now she had no control, and she liked that. She trusted it. She gave it all to this drug, whatever it was. It could have her. All her problems, all her wants and needs—she was sick of her life.

This was sweet.

She had only one thought: life would be good indeed if she had enough of this powder on hand to have a taste of it whenever she wanted. Fuck booze. To hell with Valium. This was for her. This was the best.

*This* was living.

The visual image of those six big bricks in the next room made her smile, at least she felt as if her face might be smiling. She wasn't sure. She didn't care.

She closed her eyes and listened to a symphony orchestra tune up, and she watched reel one of the movie of her life unfold on the wide screen of her mind.

~ ~ ~

Neither Richard nor Natalie heard the glass in the kitchen door break, nor did they hear the muffled footsteps and muted whispers of the two airport baggage handlers as they nervously, yet methodically, searched the house for a black suitcase that had they had somehow let slip through their system.

# Chapter 6

About the time that Lorenzo and Sweetann were heading for the zoo to meet up with Spike, and airport baggage handlers were sneaking in through Richard and Natalie's kitchen door, Nicky was grabbed up out of his bed by a strong man covering his mouth.

At first, he felt disoriented, and wasn't sure if he was awake, or if this was the most awful nightmare he'd ever had, or what. But then he smelled the leather of the man's glove and smelled the man's bad breath and he knew this was no dream.

"Shut up or I'll kill you," the man said. Nicky nodded. Nicky was no idiot. He knew about bad guys from watching television, and he knew that he had to be smart and not make himself a victim. "I want you to get dressed. Fast and quiet, okay?"

Nicky nodded again, his ear pressed hard against the man's chest, hurting his jaw and his neck. His heart was beating like it wanted to escape his chest, and he couldn't breathe because of the man's glove over his mouth and part of his nose.

He started to struggle. He didn't want to, but he couldn't breathe.

The man released him, and Nicky sucked in a long, ragged breath and moved his head around on a wrenched neck.

"Now," the man said quietly. "Dressed."

Emergency, Nicky thought. Here it is. He wondered if Charlotte was calling her mom. What an idiot.

Remember everything, he told himself. Writers—playwrights—notice details. Some day he'd be a writer, a playwright. Some day he'd write about this.

Nicky's Mariner's t-shirt and jeans were still on the chair where he'd thrown them the night before. He pulled off his pajamas and got into them, trying not to look at the guy who sat on the bed watching him dress. "What about Charlotte?" he asked.

"Shut up," the man said.

While he was dressing, he snuck looks at the guy. His face

reminded Nicky of some cartoon character he couldn't exactly remember. Somebody with a really long face and square, crooked, horsey teeth.

Nicky tied his shoes, and when he was finished, the guy stood up and grabbed his arm and jerked him toward the door.

"Hey," Nicky protested. "I'm coming. You don't have to do that."

"Shut the fuck up," the man said.

In the living room, Charlotte stood rigidly still, wearing her yellow nightie, her bare feet stuck into sneakers that hadn't been tied. Another man, a smaller, darker haired, darker skinned man held on to her.

"Jesus," the man who held Nicky said. "She can't go out like that."

"She wouldn't get dressed."

"Not with you watching me," she said.

Nicky felt admiration for Charlotte's guts, even though she was stupid to defy them, and his fear was so strong he could taste the bitterness of it on the back of his tongue.

"Why do we want to take her, anyway?" the dark man said.

Horseteeth shrugged. "Can't just leave her."

Nicky remembered the phone call earlier from that guy named William. His mom had never mentioned anybody named William before; he would have remembered that because his best friend's name was William. Maybe this was the guy who called. This was definitely not a friend of his mom's.

This was Fagan.

No! Worse! This was Bill Sikes, the really bad guy from *Oliver Twist*, the play Nicky was going to audition for next month.

*William Sikes! That's what he should have told his mom.*

Horseteeth gave Nicky a shove toward the little guy and then he grabbed Charlotte. They both must have sensed that Nicky wasn't going to give them any trouble. The little guy pushed Nick down into a chair and stood over him with a hand pressing down on his shoulder. Horseteeth pulled Charlotte back into the bedroom.

"I'll scream," she said. "I swear to God I'll scream."

"If you scream—" the man said, and then his words were

lost as they closed the bedroom door.

All the warnings his mother had given him about strange men approaching him at school, on the street, in the mall, hit him full force and fear boiled up and heated his face.

Bill Sikes.

"What's happening here?" Nicky asked.

"We're going on a trip," the man said. "We're going to go visit your mom."

That didn't sound right, none of it sounded right, but Nicky was a kid, and he wasn't supposed to know everything. He didn't think they were going to hurt him, he hoped Charlotte would do what they wanted so they wouldn't hurt her, either. If they were taking them to see his mom, then they probably wouldn't hurt either one of them.

He heard protests coming from the bedroom, but they were not loud, so Nicky didn't think he needed to take any action. He was glad, because he didn't know what he would do. A few minutes later, Charlotte came out wearing the jeans and sweater she'd had on the night before, and had her tennis shoes in her hand. Her hair was messed up, and she was scared.

Nick looked at her and had a bad feeling in his stomach that things weren't going to go well for Charlotte. She was too young. She was only fifteen and kind of stupid. Mom should have found someone else to stay with him for the weekend. Charlotte was okay as a babysitter if nothing went wrong, but now something had gone wrong, and she was not a good one to be in charge.

She held her hand out to Nicky, who took it. He knew it was a gesture that she hoped would calm him, but she was clearly the one who needed to be reassured. He gave her hand an extra squeeze.

"C'mon, kids," Horseteeth said. "Let's go for a ride."

# Chapter 7

Boingo's cell phone vibrated in his pocket just as that old rich fart Harrison raised his bet.

Table rules in the private game behind Club Rocco said no cell phones, so he had to ignore it, but he couldn't concentrate on the game if he was worried about who was calling him at this inconvenient hour.

He looked down at his stack of chips. He was ahead at the moment, but not by much. Boingo knew Harrison, and knew how he bet. Most of all, he had a pretty good feeling that Harrison wasn't bluffing this hand.

Boingo had a six and eight of diamonds in the hole, and the flop had been a seven of spades, and a four and a ten of hearts. All he needed was a five or a nine and he'd rake in a big mother pot.

But inside straights were elusive. It was a crazy, desperate bet.

Harrison likely had a pair in the hole. Maybe he flopped two pair, or three of a kind. Harrison had that "come and get me" look on his face that Boingo hated.

*Who the hell was calling him?*

Boingo had hoped that Harrison would fold once he raised, but Harrison countered with even a bigger raise.

Boingo had shit.

He threw his cards to the dealer. "Gotta piss," he said, and stood up from the table, as Harrison reached across with both hands to rake in a monster pot.

Boingo walked out through the door into the bar, the music loud and pounding. Girls in sparkly g-strings danced on a raised platform ringed by tables filled with guys drinking twenty-dollar beers and yelling at the girls.

He stopped for a moment to see if Harmony was dancing. She gave the best lap dances ever. If she was on the floor tonight, Boingo just might cash in his chips and tuck his meager winnings into her g-string.

He pushed his way into the stinking men's room, pulled

out his phone and checked the message.

"Boingo, I need you to stand by." The voice was cold and efficient, as always. "I may have an errand for you to do for me tonight. Stay sober, keep your phone on, and expect a call. Be ready to move."

As always, Boingo had a debt to pay. He knew that if he was ever going to repay any debts at all, he better start with this one. Maybe just standing by was good enough, but he didn't want to push it. He needed to just suck it up and run whatever inconvenient little errand they wanted him to run, and then be done with those guys. For good.

He put the phone back in his pocket, then made a decision.

Back in the poker room, he held up his hands. "I'm cashing out," he said.

Nobody protested. He wasn't leaving with much of their money, and usually they had all of his money by the time he left.

"I might have a job tonight."

He collected his chips and took them to the guy in the corner, who counted them out, then exchanged the stacks for a small wad of bills.

"Bye," he said, but nobody responded.

He saw Harmony as soon as he went back into the bar. He motioned her over, and took the wad of bills from his pocket, and then decided against it. The idea of that phone ringing at any moment jerking him into instant action was going to mess with his concentration. He wouldn't want to put Harmony through that. He'd come back when he could relax and really enjoy her talents.

He tucked a twenty into her g-string. "See you, gorgeous."

She whined a little, and his hands itched to reach out and touch her, but he'd only had to make that mistake once to learn the rules of Club Rocco.

Instead, he went home and stared into the dark corners of his little apartment and thought of the big time hoods who had long ago hooked him up with the small weed distribution he ran. What it must be like to have the kind of power that they had. They had the power to take away his poker game. They had enough power to disolve his sleep. They had enough power to squelch a hard on. They had enough power to make him nervous from very far away with only the threat of an errand.

Crap.

Boingo sighed and lit another smoke. This was going to be a long night.

## Chapter 8

Sweetann's feeling of unreality vanished with a stab of fear as they got back into the car and Lorenzo started talking about leaving everything, her whole life behind and running from the bad guys. Running hard, running fast, running forever.

Uprooting Nicky. Jerking him out of his play, out of his school, away from his friends.

Was this worth it?

"How much money are we talking about?" she asked.

"I don't know, babe."

"Well, it makes a difference." She looked down at her hands in her lap. "I'm so tired, Lorenzo." The admission escaped before she could stop it. "I'm so tired of being poor all the time. It isn't fair to Nicky. I work so hard. I work long hours, we spend nothing, and I just fall deeper and deeper into debt. Last year Nicky got two thrift store t-shirts for his birthday, and I found a cake mix at half price. No frosting." She felt the flush of shame creep up her throat. She'd never admitted that to anybody before. Nicky was so great about it. He never once complained about their poverty.

"The higher the risk the greater the reward," Lorenzo said. "You may be broke, but you're safe."

"I'm so sick of it. I'm so sick of doing it all alone. Alone and broke. It's a lot to raise a kid alone. I'm just so tired." She was afraid she was going to cry, and that's not what she wanted to do in front of Lorenzo. She was sorry she'd started the 'poor me' thing. That wasn't how she wanted Lorenzo to see her. That wasn't how she wanted anybody to see her. That's one of the reasons she was so tired—she worked so hard just to keep up the appearance that they were middle class. The low end of middle class to be sure, but not poor. They were not poor people and she would not raise Nicky to have poverty mentality. "This money could make a difference. A real difference."

Lorenzo drove quietly.

"Are you afraid?" she asked.

"Scared to fucking death."

That admission did nothing to allay her fears. "Whatever happens, big guy," she said, "I trust your instincts. You call the shots."

A tiny smile crossed his lips. "Want to jump into the back seat?"

"Yes," she said. "But not quite yet." She put one hand on his bicep. It was big and hard. "Soon."

His smile turned into a grin. "Good. I'm going to need to release some tension pretty soon."

"Oh the romance in your soul," she said. "That's what I love about you."

Lorenzo's face turned grim as he turned a corner. "Whenever you want to stop and throw that suitcase back at the bad guys, sweetie, you just say the word."

"For now, let's keep our options open."

"They're closing."

"I know."

Sweetann wondered if that little statement she'd just made was going to seal her fate. Would she never see her apartment again? Would she never step foot into her office? Would she never see Seattle again? Her brother?

Nicky?

Was he going to be all right?

Maybe she should call him.

No, it was late, and he had rehearsal tomorrow. Of course he was going to be all right.

Anything else was not an option.

Could she settle down in Rio and make a life with Lorenzo and Nicky? Was this worth it? Wouldn't it be better to just muddle along at her bottom-level government job until retirement? This big score thing was not real. It couldn't be real.

Could it?

It happened to other people, didn't it? Giant windfalls right out of nowhere? It could happen to her. If anybody deserved it. . . .

Jeez, what a concept.

*Don't start believing that you deserve this,* she told herself. *This is drug money and don't you ever forget it.*

A touch of nausea began to bloom in her belly.

*Your escalating debt is your fault, and you have no right to think someone else needs to pay it. Not your parents' estate, not Richard and Natalie, not even Nicky's absentee father. You made your decisions, you do right by them. All of them.*

Lorenzo made a right turn, cut off the lights and coasted to a stop in what looked like a deserted area of town. Old warehouses stood bleak and gray, dingy and gritty.

"Where are we?" she whispered, happy to have something distract her from her own thoughts that fueled her escalating panic.

"It's what they call the zoo. I want you to get on the floor in the back seat and cover yourself with a blanket or something. Take a nap."

"Hell, no."

"Don't argue with me, Sweetann. This is not a day at the park. These guys play rough. If I'm going to get cut, I don't want them to even know you exist."

"Give it up. I'm going with you."

"I should take you back to the house. You're going to ruin it."

"I'm going with you." She crossed her arms over her chest.

"Fuck," Lorenzo said. He put his chin on the top of the steering wheel and stared out into the night. He seemed to come to a conclusion moments later, though, because he took a deep breath and looked at her. "All right. Stay close to me and *say nothing*. You got that? Say *nothing.*"

"I heard you." Sweetann wanted to crack a joke of some kind, or get a quick kiss for luck, just to throw a little normalcy into this bizarre situation, but Lorenzo was strung pretty tight and she didn't want to push him. Maybe he needed to concentrate. Instead, she got out of the car and followed his lead of closing the door quietly. The advantage of a class car like a BMW was that the doors didn't have to be slammed. They merely clicked closed. They'd never be able to pull this off if they were driving her ancient Ford.

She had to take a step and a half to each of his long-legged ones, and her mind, eager to be somewhere else, wondered if his shoes lasted twice as long as hers did since he took half as many steps.

They stopped at a warehouse side door. Sweetann could see a light upstairs, a faint yellow glow through the crusty window. Lorenzo tried the knob. Locked. He knocked three times, loud.

Sweetann heard her heart pounding in the ensuing silence. Then footsteps scuffed along the warehouse floor, and a voice on the other side said, "Yeah?"

"It's Lorenzo. I'm looking for Spike."

"Just a minute." Footsteps faded, then a moment later, returned. The door opened and a young blonde kid with tattoos and an attitude stood there.

"Spike's upstairs," he said. He looked at Sweetann. "Think I better entertain your friend here. Spike don't like strangers."

"She's with me," Lorenzo said. "Spike isn't going to like it if you make me go away."

The kid looked Sweetann up and down in an exaggerated-asshole way. "Okay," he said. "I'm not much interested anyway."

Sweetann wanted to pop him one, but she stayed silent, and walked a couple of steps behind Lorenzo. She definitely wanted to be in the background. This was like a bad movie.

Maybe that's how she ought to begin thinking of it. Like she's been cast in a B-movie with two-bit hoods like that kid, right out of Central Casting.

The warehouse was empty except for a half dozen crates on pallets stacked in the corner. The place smelled like wet concrete and dust. Unused. Stairs led to a second floor office. Sweetann could see the back of a man's head through the office window. She followed Lorenzo up the wooden stairs, looking around for the nearest exit.

"Lorenzo!" A youngish guy, black hair slicked back, with sharp eyes, thin lips and badly capped front teeth smiled too widely at him, then shook Lorenzo's hand and slapped him on the back. "Haven't seen you in years, buddy, years. Where you been hanging out?" He eyed Sweetann, and without waiting for Lorenzo's answer to his rhetorical question, said, "And who's this, the missus?"

"This is Lois," Lorenzo said. "A friend." He smiled encouragement at her. "This is Spike."

They shook hands, Spike gazing into her eyes and holding her hand two beats too long.

Sweetann wasn't fooled. She knew he wasn't attracted to her. This was establishing pecker order. If she hadn't been so freaked out with fear over what they were doing, she'd find it humorous. Maybe they'd laugh about it later.

Maybe not.

Spike sat in an old gray squeaky swivel chair behind an old, scarred, World War II gray metal desk and put the heel of his tennis shoe up on the corner of it. He gestured toward two metal folding chairs and Lorenzo and Sweetann sat down. The blonde kid left the room, closing the door behind him. Sweetann began to relax. This was no big deal. This Spike guy and his sidekick were just punks. Nicky could have written this script. Neither one of them was over thirty. She and Lorenzo could handle them with their egos tied behind their backs.

"Charles said you had the airport shipment," he said.

Sweetann twitched in surprise, but Lorenzo was smooth as silk. "That's right," he said as he settled back in the chair.

"Dirty shit, Lorenzo."

"I want to move it fast."

"I bet you do." Spike moved a cell phone closer to him, and tapped his fingers on top of it. "Got a taste?"

Lorenzo pulled his wallet from his back pocket and extracted one of the tiny, brightly colored envelopes. Sweetann didn't have her glasses on, but if she did, she'd bet this one had pink bikini panties on it. He held it between two fingers and made Spike sit up and reach for it.

Spike took his time unfolding it very carefully. When it sat open on the desk, the powder in a crease, he wet a forefinger, dabbed it in the powder, then tasted it. "Fuck. Me," he said.

Lorenzo replaced his wallet and sat back. "Fast," he said. "I want to move this fast."

Spike looked at the two of them with what could possibly be a tiny bit more respect, picked up the cell phone and punched in a speed-dial number. "The airport's at the zoo," he said, then hung up. He pulled a dollar bill from his shirt pocket and rolled it up, all the time looking back and forth between Lorenzo and Sweetann. "They're on to you already, you know."

"Yeah, well, maybe, and maybe not," Lorenzo said. "What kind of time frame are we talking about here?"

"How fast could you get it here?"

"For the right price? Twenty minutes."

Spike put one end of the rolled up bill in his nostril and the other in the paper and snorted the remaining powder.

"Relax," he said. "It's going to be a few minutes before they get here."

"Who?" Sweetann said, then wished she'd shut up, just like Lorenzo said.

Spike grinned at her, showing the black gums that outlined his bad caps. "The big boys," he said, his voice already a touch slower and lower because of the drug. He leaned back again in the chair and this time put both feet on the desk. "So where you been keeping yourself, Lorenzo?"

"Been keeping straight."

Spike looked like he wanted to laugh, but no longer had the energy. "Straight, eh? Yeah, that's what I ought to be." His eyelids lowered.

"Six years," Lorenzo added.

"Ha," Spike said, but there was no mirth in his voice. He closed his eyes. "Some good shit," he said, then appeared to fall asleep.

Lorenzo looked at Sweetann and rolled his eyes. Sweetann was glad Lorenzo wasn't like this bozo. He may have been at one time, but he wasn't any more, and she liked that. She liked that a lot. She reached over and touched his knee.

"Huh?" Spike said, jerking awake, opening his eyes, then closing them and relaxing.

Lorenzo put his big hand over Sweetann's small one. "We just wait," he whispered.

They didn't wait long. Sweetann heard the door open downstairs, and male voices. Lorenzo stood up and looked out the window. "It's Pete," he said, "and somebody else. Oh crap."

Sweetann stood up and looked down into the warehouse where the blonde kid was talking with two guys in dark suits. "What?"

"It's The Cook."

"Cook? Which?"

"The tall thin guy."

Sweetann saw the blonde kid shake hands with the two

men, then pointed up at them. The two men looked up and Sweetann felt a chill run down her back. So these were the big boys, according to Spike. They certainly made Lorenzo nervous. For a moment, she wished she hadn't come. She wished she had just taken that damned suitcase back to the airport and been done with it. She had a feeling that this was the step that went over the line. She knew there would be no going back once those men entered this room.

She touched Lorenzo's arm. "What about Spike?" They both looked at him, nodded off in his chair, feet on the desk.

Lorenzo shrugged.

Heavy footsteps resounded through the wooden room. They turned together to face the door.

"Lorenzo," Pete said as he opened the door. He shook Lorenzo's hand. "Long time."

"Hi, Pete."

Pete, about forty, took Sweetann's hand and kissed her fingers. His hand was soft and warm. Sweetann decided she liked Pete, with his pudgy features and kind smile. He wore small round glasses and looked like a banker.

"Lorenzo," The Cook said, taking Lorenzo's hand. He nodded to Sweetann. "Don't tell me," he said. "You must be Sweetann Holt."

Sweetann felt her mouth go dry in the face of his authority. The Cook was in charge. He was tall, thin, with a long nose and dark eyes. His dark hair was slicked back, though gray showed at the temples. Probably fifty-ish. He wore his suit like a department store mannequin.

"From Seattle. You're rude to not introduce us, Lorenzo." He fixed his stare on her and Sweetann felt pegged to the floor. "How's Nicky?" He didn't wait for an answer; he didn't shake hands.

Sweetann felt as though he had his long, aristocratic fingers around Nicky's throat, and she wanted to let him have everything. She wanted to run, to grab Lorenzo and run. What on earth had she been thinking? No amount of money was worth this. Lorenzo had been right to want her to stay in the car. She could be his downfall.

"What the fuck is this?" The Cook said, gesturing at Spike.

"Huh?" Spike said, his eyelids opening, his eyes rolling. He saw The Cook and his arms flew up, tipping his chair back and over. "Fuck," he said, scrambling up from the floor and righting the chair. "You guys surprised me."

The Cook reached a finely manicured hand over and picked up the folded paper. He flicked the rolled dollar bill onto the floor and Spike had to scramble around on the floor under the desk to retrieve it. "How is it, Spike?"

Spike pocketed the bill, stood up, scratched his nose, ran his fingers through his hair. "Best I've tasted," he said, looking down at the scarred desktop.

"Good. You can go now."

Spike didn't hesitate, clearly happy to get out of there with his skin on. It was a weird feeling, standing within the aura of so much power. These flunkies gave The Cook his power, that was true, but he knew how to wield it, too. He commanded it. And she wasn't immune.

"That kid," The Cook said. He walked around to the back of the desk, sat down in the chair and leaned back, comfortable in his power. "That kid. I invest in him and he continually disappoints me. He's going nowhere, know what I mean?" He leaned forward and pushed the opened envelope around on the desk. "He's a small time punk and he'll end up dead, know why? Because of this shit. If you only deal in it you can do well. But if you begin to put it in your veins..." he stopped and looked at Lorenzo. "Hey, what am I lecturing you for?"

"Six years clean and sober, Cookie," Lorenzo said.

The Cook leaned back again, appraising Lorenzo with a fresh eye. "I'm going to get the kid downstairs to come up here and pat you two down," he said. "You don't object, do you?" He looked at Sweetann.

"You don't have to—" Lorenzo said.

"Oh, but I do," he said, steepling his long fingers. "Those airport guys have been trying to break my balls for a long time now. If they sent you here, this would be just the thing that would get me a bullet through my eye." He looked up and nodded at Pete. Pete opened the door and summoned the blonde kid.

Sweetann's sphincter tightened. This guy had his power

trip down good.

"Now remember," The Cook said to the blonde kid when he showed up. "Those radio transmitters can be very, very tiny."

The kid gave Lorenzo a cursory pat down, then he turned to Sweetann and grinned scummy teeth at her. She closed her eyes and stood quietly while his hands went slowly over her entire body, lingering on her breasts, tweaking her nipples, squeezing her buttocks, fingering her crotch. When he was finished, he had a massive hard on showing through his jeans and Sweetann found it difficult indeed to keep from slapping him or kicking him or bursting into tears. It humiliated her, and that's exactly what The Cook wanted.

She chanced a glance at Lorenzo, whose face was beet red as he stood still, and she knew it was perhaps harder on him. She swallowed and got her control back.

"They're clean, boss," he said, grinning at Sweetann. She stood as if at attention, looking straight ahead, ignoring him.

"Get out," The Cook said to the kid. "Sit down," he said to Lorenzo and Sweetann. They sat down again on the beat up metal folding chairs like well-trained puppies. "How much do you have? All of it?"

"All of it. Six kilos."

"How fast can you get it here?"

"What's the price?"

"You'll take what I give you, Lorenzo. I suppose the stuff is at Natalie and Richard's house, and it would take my men about thirty seconds to go in and get it. Natalie and Richard might get hurt in the process, though, and none of us want that. The airport guys will be at that house in about twenty minutes anyway, so this is your one and only chance. Give me the goods, I'll give you guys enough money to get out of town and we've done good business together. If you dilly-dally around, then my men will get the goods, not pay you a fucking penny, and the airport thugs will kill Nicky." He sat back in the chair again. "Sorry to paint such an ugly picture, Sweetann, but you folks chose the low road."

"Okay," Lorenzo said, and Sweetann breathed a sigh of relief. "We'll go get it. You have the cash?"

The Cook smiled a shark's smile, and said, "Trust me."

"Let's go."

"Leave Sweetann here with me," The Cook said.

"No," Sweetann said. She gripped Lorenzo's hand.

"I insist you be my guest."

Pete moved in front of the door.

"No way," Lorenzo said. "Sweetann comes with me. We're a pair."

In one tiny compartment of her mind, the place where life was normal, Sweetann got a pleasant girlish thrill out of that. A moment later, reality returned.

The Cook sighed. "You've got sixteen minutes," he said looking at his watch. "Go."

Pete moved out of the way, Lorenzo pushed Sweetann out the door and they ran down the stairs, past the blonde kid, out the other door and they danced with itchy urgency in the cool night as Lorenzo fumbled the keys to the BMW.

They jumped into the car, Lorenzo fired it up and they peeled out of the ugly neighborhood.

"How do they all know about me and Nick, Lorenzo?" Sweetann asked. "How the hell do they *all* know about my boy?"

"I don't know, Sweets," Lorenzo said. "The internet, maybe. Who knows? They have ways of getting information, that's all."

"I hate it."

"Yeah. Me, too." He put a comforting hand on her knee. "Do you have a girlfriend at home you trust? Like someone you would trust with your life?"

"Patty."

"Okay. I'm going to stop at the Seven-Eleven. You go call Patty, tell her to pick up Nicky and take him to the train station."

"I've got my cell."

"No cell phones. Use the pay phone."

Sweetann didn't know how powerful The Cook was, but she had a feeling he had tentacles that reached around the globe. This seemed like a prudent move. "Why the train station?"

"We're going to go get Natalie and Richard and the suitcase. I'm not going to give it to Cookie for a dollar ninety-eight and I'm not going to give it back to those airport creeps, either.

We'll just get out of town, go to the desert or something, take a deep breath, all of us together, and decide what to do."

Sweetann didn't want to give the stuff to The Cook, but she didn't want to be on the run with a suitcase full of dope, either. Not with Nicky. Especially not with Nicky.

"But first," Lorenzo continued, "we get Nicky to a safe place. The train is nicely low-tech." He took a hard right and stopped at a phone booth. "Call," he said.

Patty was Sweetann's best friend in the world. They'd do anything for each other, and Sweetann was asking for just exactly that.

Patty answered with a sleepy voice. Sweetann had to talk fast and repeat things to make certain Patty was aware enough to remember it all. "Just get on the train," Sweetann told her. "Get Nicky, get on the next train to LA. Get a berth, a sleeper. And don't let him wander around by himself. I'll meet you at the station when you get here."

"This must be serious," Patty said, the sleep gone from her voice.

"Dead serious. I'll see you in LA."

It wasn't until after she hung up that she realized this screwed up their idea of behaving normally. If Patty and Nicky got on the Saturday morning train, they'd pull into LA Sunday night. So much for flying home on schedule.

She squeezed her eyes. *What was she thinking?* There was nobody to act normal for. Everybody already knew everything.

Things were moving fast. She and Lorenzo had taken one step too many. There was no going back. But maybe calling Patty was a little bit premature. They didn't have a plan. They needed a plan. Haphazard wasn't going to get them through this with their hides intact.

Speaking of which, she wanted to know how The Cook got that name, but she had a feeling she didn't want to know right this minute.

At least Nick was one step ahead of the bad guys. Patty would be there in less than ten minutes.

She could still feel that icky kid's hands on her, and her mouth involuntarily twisted up in disgust. She wanted a bath. Or, better yet, she wanted Lorenzo to make love to her, erase the bad feelings and replace them with nice feelings.

"Done," she said as she bounced back into the warm car.

"Good," he said, and they headed for Natalie and Richard's house.

Lorenzo reached over and put his hand on Sweetann's. "Some day we'll laugh about all of this," he said.

She didn't want to admit that the danger didn't seem real. Except for being felt up by that thug. "Yeah," she said, then managed a tense laugh. It broke the tension, and it was good. Lorenzo smiled, his lips tight.

Lorenzo cut the headlights as they entered the driveway and he pushed the automatic door opener. They pulled into the garage and lowered the door and killed the engine.

"Okay," Lorenzo whispered in the silence. "We go in, we grab the suitcase, we get Natalie and Richard, and we head out. We'll decide what to do, where to go and how we're going to proceed once we're all in the car and on the road. We've got two minutes, okay?"

Sweetann smiled at him. She couldn't help it. Now that Nicky was safe, this all seemed melodramatic and thrilling, in spite of the danger. Maybe it was because of the danger. She leaned over and planted a little sugar right on his lips. "Okay," she said, and they jumped out and dashed into the kitchen.

Glass crunched beneath Lorenzo's boot and they both froze.

"Fuck," he whispered, and she followed his gaze to the broken pane in the kitchen door that led to the back patio.

Now it was serious. Now it was dead serious, and Sweetann's heart began to pound. She hoped to God that whoever had broken in had done so while Natalie and Richard were out, they got the suitcase and the whole thing was over. She and Lorenzo could go upstairs and hit the sack, they'd pick Patty and Nicky up at the train station on Sunday night and go out to dinner, then after a bittersweet goodbye, she'd get on a plane with her son and her friend, and she'd have a story to tell her grandkids.

But somehow she didn't think that's how it was going to go.

"Shhh," Lorenzo said, but she knew that they made enough noise coming into the garage, what with the electric opener, that anybody in the house would know they'd come in.

Like Natalie and Richard. Where the hell were they?

Now it was so serious that Sweetann had a hard time catching her breath.

"Natalie and Richard," she whispered.

Lorenzo nodded and stepped carefully out of the glass. "Stay here," he whispered.

"No way," she said, remembering for just an instant that the last time she said that, some greasy blonde kid got his fingers on her privates.

She followed him out of the kitchen, and through the living room. Nothing seemed to be out of order; except the unearthly quiet. Natalie and Richard should be here. Their Bronco was in the garage, the lights were on. Cups, glasses, scissors and a Victoria's Secret catalogue were on the coffee table where they'd been when Sweetann and Lorenzo took off in the Beamer. Sweetann squeezed her eyes shut and prayed that they weren't upstairs with their throats slashed.

No sooner had she closed her eyes than a forearm wrapped around her neck and pulled her backwards off her feet.

"Aagk," she said, her air choked off.

Lorenzo spun around and stopped as he stood.

"Get the suitcase," a low voice said next to her ear.

"Don't hurt her," he said.

"Get the fucking suitcase."

"Okay." He held his hands up. "Okay. Sweetann, you all right?"

He released the pressure a little; she gulped air, nodded, fought hard against passing out. She saw globes of colors floating in her periphery, her heart hammered so loudly she was afraid it would burst.

*Please just give them the suitcase,* she prayed. *Please don't kill me, I've got a little boy.*

Lorenzo took the stairs two at a time and ducked into her bedroom. He came out a moment later, the suitcase in one hand, his other hand up in plain sight.

"That's it," she heard another voice say, then a man in a ski mask took the suitcase from Lorenzo. "Lie down over in the corner there."

Lorenzo did as he was told. "Sweetann, you all right?"

"She's fine," the voice next to her ear said. "Okay, honey, you go lie down on top of him," and he gave her a shove.

She looked back and both of them were wearing jeans and sweatshirts, Nikes and black ski masks. She lay down on top of Lorenzo's back, and wished she was back in her tiny apartment and her boring job, pinching pennies with her wonderful son.

"We're leaving now. If I see either one of you before we drive out of here, Nicky dies. Got that?"

It was like a stab through Sweetann's heart. She nodded, still gasping for breath, knowing that as soon as those jerks were gone, she would start to cry.

She closed her eyes, felt Lorenzo breathing beneath her. She heard footsteps grind glass, then the kitchen door opened and closed.

She rolled off him and he took her in his long arms.

Over. It was all over.

She held him close, relief flushing through her. This had been a stupid way to spend the evening. What a ridiculous risk they had taken. Fortunately, the angels were with them, or God was smiling down or something, because it was over and they were all still all right. All the tension of the last few hours ran out of her, leaving her feeling limp and exhausted.

"You okay?"

She nodded against his chest.

"C'mon, then. We've got to hurry."

"What? Why?" She looked at him. He seemed just as intense as he did a few minutes ago. Adrenaline spurted through her again. "What?"

"Get Natalie and Richard. And get the fuck out of here before they discover your underwear."

"No, Lorenzo, you didn't..." Shock flushed through her, she felt the blood drain from her face. She was stunned. She was beyond anger and into speechless outrage.

"Yep. Let's go." He got up and pulled her to her feet. She wanted to slap him. She wanted to kick him. Pound him.

Instead, she followed him up the stairs.

At first, she thought Natalie and Richard were dead. They were on their backs on their bed, their eyes closed.

Then she saw the rolled up hundred-dollar bill in the dish

on the bed between them.

"Fuck," Lorenzo said. "They got loaded."

Richard opened his eyes. "Hey," he said softly. Natalie cracked her eyes open and closed them again.

"C'mon, you guys, we've got to get out of here."

Natalie made a tiny whining sound.

"Go away," Richard whispered, then closed his eyes again.

"I'm not kidding." Lorenzo grabbed Richard's arm and pulled him up.

"Hey," he said weakly.

"Get her up," Lorenzo ordered Sweetann, and her anger redirected from Lorenzo's stupidity to Natalie's. She wanted to slap Natalie silly. Instead, she grabbed Natalie's arm and hauled her to a sitting position.

Natalie began to gag.

Lorenzo took the suitcase and Richard down to the BMW while Sweetann hustled Natalie into the bathroom then held her head over the toilet as she vomited up everything in her flat, highly-toned stomach.

"Come *on*," Lorenzo said, his head poking into the harsh light of the bathroom.

"We're coming," Sweetann said, angry at everything, especially herself, especially at stupid Natalie. She held Natalie's head up by a handful of her hair. Sweetann wet a washcloth, tipped Natalie's face up, wiped it, then helped her to her feet. She waited while Natalie rinsed her mouth in slow motion, then, feeling as itchy as Lorenzo acted, she grabbed two designer towels from the master bathroom just in case this wasn't the end of the puking, and hustled her stumbling sister-in-law down the stairs and into the car.

"Good way to treat a drinking problem, Natalie," Sweetann couldn't help but saying, but Natalie wasn't hearing her.

By the time they had backed out of the driveway and the garage door was closed, Natalie and Richard were slumped over onto each other in the back seat, eyes closed. Sweetann threw the towels into their laps.

"Well," Lorenzo breathed a sigh of relief and squeezed Sweetann's knee. She wasn't sure she wanted him to touch her.

"So far, so good."

She wanted to smack him.

# Chapter 9

Lorenzo knew he had gone over the line. Way over the line. Now here he was, driving like a maniac in somebody else's BMW, two stoned idiots in the back seat, a trunk full of heroin and cash and an innocent woman next to him with thugs after her little boy. Damn. He better do some fast thinking and his hunches better be along the right lines.

He could always make a left turn and take the suitcase to The Cook. That was always an option.

No, it wasn't. Cookie wouldn't pay them enough to be able to escape the airport thugs, who would probably gleefully kill them all for stealing their stash.

Those kids in the ski masks—they were from the airport. One of them recognized the suitcase immediately. So now, because of Lorenzo's good idea, there were *two* sets of bad guys after them.

Shit.

He jumped on the freeway and headed east. The traffic was light at—he looked at the digital clock—1:47 a.m. He set the cruise control for two mph under the limit and sat back.

Sweetann was fuming next to him; he could feel her vibes. He couldn't blame her. He'd made an inexcusable, reckless move, endangering everybody, especially Sweetann's son. He didn't know what to say to her. There was nothing to say. He'd been caught up in the romance of the Big Score. He may be clean and sober, but once a junkie, always a junkie.

Fuck.

When they were well out of the city, Lorenzo knew where to go. The idea came suddenly, and along with it came a stomachache. It was a terrible idea, but as personally uncomfortable as it might be, it was the safest spot possible.

He'd take these two smacked up jerks and a suitcase of heroin to his Narcotics Anonymous sponsor's house.

Jack wasn't home, he was filming on location in London, but Lorenzo knew where he kept the key to the guest house.

Within fifteen minutes, fifteen silent, tense minutes, he

pulled up in the drive, entered the code and watched the gate slide open.

He parked, turned off the car and they sat in the dark. In the quiet. After a long pause, Sweetann spoke.

"What is this place?"

"Friend's house."

She nodded, looking at what she could of Jack's sprawling estate. "Nice friends."

Lorenzo nodded at the darkened guesthouse straight ahead. "That's where I got clean," he said. "I spent some bad days detoxing in there."

He looked over at Sweetann, and her shiny eyes glinted in the darkness. "A long time ago," he said, then smiled at her. "A lifetime or more ago." She smiled back, uncertainly. "C'mon. Let's go knock on the door."

Lorenzo knocked on the door and breathed a silent prayer of thanks to the god who looked over reformed druggies, that someone else wasn't jonesing at Jack's place. He opened the door and hustled everyone in.

By the time they were safely inside, with deadbolts thrown, all the jostling had put Natalie back into the bathroom with dry heaves. Richard was sprawled on the couch, Sweetann sat on the edge of a chair, Lorenzo paced. The black suitcase sat in the middle of the living room where they all had to walk around it, literally as well as metaphorically.

"First things first," Sweetann said. "We all need toothbrushes."

A surge of affection came up through Lorenzo. He stood up and checked the kitchen. "Yes. And something to drink. Iced tea. Get like a case of it."

"I'm not going by myself," she said.

Lorenzo nodded toward Richard, who sat with his head back and his eyes closed. "I don't think we ought to leave these two here by themselves."

"I don't want to go to any convenience store to buy provisions with hundred dollar bills."

She had a point, and he didn't want to ask her if she had any cash. He knew his wallet was flat. "Okay. We'll make do until morning. Then everybody will be a little more refreshed," he nodded at Richard, who had begun to snore. "We can go to a drug store."

They got Richard up, pulled out the hide-a-bed, and let Richard fall back onto it. Lorenzo had done that many, many times before for friends. Worse, he had been on the accepting side of such treatment often enough when he was bouncing along, scraping bottom, trying desperately to get clean, but unable to get find his way there.

Sweetann got a disheveled, mumbling and mascara-smudged Natalie cleaned up and down on the bed next to her husband. Though they could pass for drunk, Lorenzo knew they weren't, and it was a bit of a frightening thing to see. They'd just tooted a little of the stuff, too. He'd have shot it in his veins and been zonked like that for years. This was good for him to see. It was a good reminder of a terrible existence, and a nice bright contrast to his current moderate, boring, satisfying life.

"Not pretty, are they?" Sweetann said.

Understatement, Lorenzo thought.

Natalie and Richard were both snoring before Lorenzo turned out the lights and put his arms around Sweetann.

She hugged him back, laid her head on his chest. "I hate you," she said.

"I know. I'm sorry."

"I'm not kidding, Lorenzo." She pulled back and looked into his eyes. "Look what you've done. You could have stopped all this."

"You said you were going to let me call the shots." He felt like a jerk for trying to justify his bad behavior. More junkie behavior on top of junkie behavior.

"Well, that was a dumb call."

"Maybe."

"No maybe. Dumb call." She put her head back on his chest. "I'm just so tired," she said. "All over again, I'm tired. I'm tired and I'm scared. I'm scared half to death."

"I'm sorry," he said.

She pulled back and looked at him in the dim light. "Who *are* you, anyway, Lorenzo? I thought I had an idea of who you were, a cute, funny guy with a past, but maybe I was wrong about all that."

Thank God she didn't know the ways of the drug culture. Thank God she didn't know how that shit got into your head as well as your bloodstream and never, ever left. Thank God she and her boy had never had to deal with someone like him before. He'd like to protect her from ever having to know too much about it. About him.

"Shhh," he said.

"I mean who knows guys named The Cook, and knows about places like the zoo and that horrible bar?"

He put a finger to her lips. "I'm not a nice guy, Sweetann. I've done a lot of bad things in my life–things I hope you never even have to imagine."

"Tell me."

He shook his head. "I don't even want to think about some of them. I try to live like all that is behind me, but now, this. This takes me back to when I was a criminal, and I'm finding myself thinking and acting in those same grooved channels."

"*Tell me*," she insisted.

"Maybe some day you'll know more than you ever wanted to."

She put her cheek back against his chest.

"Come lie down with me," he said, and began walking her backward toward the bedroom.

"I want to take a quick shower," she said.

"Good idea." He pivoted, swinging her around in front of him, and waddled her into the bathroom.

"No," she said.

"Yes."

"What?" she asked, smiling up at him. She clearly didn't want to smile, but couldn't help herself.

"Me shower too," he said. God, she was adorable. Had he ever noticed how adorable she was?

"No," she said.

"Yes," he said, and got the water running. Then he turned off the bathroom light and began to undress her. Sweater off, he knelt on the floor and unzipped her jeans, then pressed his face against her soft belly. "I need you," he whispered.

She put both hands on his face and brought him back up to

his feet for a soft kiss. "I need you, too," she whispered. Soon they were soaped up and sliding around each other in the spray, his soapy cock between her legs, sliding back and forth as they kissed and she ran her hands in circles on the lathered up hair on his chest.

She had those small, perfectly formed breasts, tiny things with big, standup nipples. He loved those. He loved her heavy rear end, too, and grabbed two fistfuls of butt and picked her up. His penis was poised and ready.

"Not yet," she said, and though he ached to slide right into her, soap and all, he set her back down and they got busy with rinsing off.

They dried each other in the dark, giggling and tripping, banging into each other and hard-edged bathroom things, then they wrapped up in towels and ran for the bedroom. Lorenzo whipped open the wall of curtains and swarms of tiny, garden fairy lights illuminated Sweetann's wet hair and passion-swollen lips.

He lay her down, unwrapped her like a birthday present, sucked one of those luscious breasts into his mouth and let his fingers prepare his way. She was ready.

"God, you're so wet," he said.

"Been that way since I first saw you tonight," she breathed into his ear, and with a practiced aim, he slid inside her, gratified at her tiny squeal of pleasure. He moved back and forth, knowing he would gladly die for this feeling, and when she caught his rhythm, the two of them moved as one, maximizing pleasure, their mouths and tongues locked together.

Then she breathed, "Oh, Lorenzo," and before he knew it, he was over the top, his mind exploding, his body dissolving. There was only his heart hammering, and somewhere in the back of his mind's eye, that suitcase, that suitcase full of power, and this woman, this sweet woman with the perfect-mouthful breasts. Then there were his genitals again, soft and somehow shameful, and he slipped from her, rolled onto his side, cupped her belly in his hand and kissed the back of her neck.

"Oh, man," she said. "I'd forgotten how much I need that." But he didn't even know if she'd come, and he felt like an insensitive lout.

It had to do with that suitcase. He felt as though he'd jacked off and come all over that fucking thing instead of making love to Sweetann.

"You're so sweet," he said, "so luscious." His fingers found one nutty little nipple and massaged it gently.

She rolled over and melted into his arms, kissing his chest, and with his chin on the top of her head, his eyes closed.

~ ~ ~

She moved and Lorenzo's eyes popped open. He raised his head and looked at the red digital numbers on the nightstand. 4:06. What did that mean? An hour of sleep?

He heard sounds in the other room, and his heart began to pound.

Bed sounds. Natalie and Richard turning over in their sleep.

Paranoia like he hadn't known since his drugging days gripped him and he found it difficult to breathe. He disentangled himself from Sweetann and the sheets, got up and stood in front of the window to the courtyard, looking out at the predawn sky. He must have been insane to get all these people into this kind of trouble.

They should keep the money, call Cookie and tell him where to pick up the dope.

No, the airport thugs would hound them for the money.

They should call the airport guys and tell them where to find the suitcase. Intact. Well, except for the eight hundred bucks Natalie suggested they lift. A good suggestion, too. Maybe they'd lift just a little bit more for the inconvenience.

Naaah, then The Cook would be on his ass.

They couldn't run, not the four of them—five, with Nicky. Not for long, anyway. They couldn't. They wouldn't.

Stash the suitcase. That was the number one priority for this morning. Stash the suitcase so only the four of them knew where it was. Then they'd deal with the airport guys and with The Cook and—

Fuck, Cookie wasn't above torturing somebody for that kind of information. How long would Natalie put up with having her fingernails broken, much less pulled out with pliers?

Maybe he should be the only one who knew where the

stuff was stashed. Maybe just he and Richard. Then maybe they could get the two warring dope peddling scumbags to bid against each other for the privilege of ownership.

He thought of Cookie in some schoolyard, showing a kid how to tie off a vein saying, "Here, kid, the first one's free." He thought of those vacant-eyed, skeletal women, opening their diseased pussies to anything for a fix. And now Lorenzo was going to profit from that, too?

For this his life as a skaghead had been spared?

Clean and sober six years, Lorenzo thought, and leaned his hot forehead against the cold glass window. And now he was about to sell his soul.

"Lorenzo?" A sleepy, tousled Sweetann sat up in bed. "You okay?"

"I'm thinking we ought to flush that stuff," he said, turning toward her.

She held one arm out to him. He walked over and took her hand.

"Good idea," she said. "Just come here."

He got back into bed next to her deliciously warm, welcoming body and realized that he needed to walk toward the warmth and the life, and not be distracted by a fast cash side trip to hell.

"Hold me," she whispered, "so I don't have to think."

He pulled her close to him, and held her while she cried, her sobs shaking the bed, her tears wetting his shoulder.

It was his fault, it was all his fault that her son was in such a dangerous position. He had made a decision that wasn't his to make, and he'd just dangled the boy over an alligator pit. Now it was up to him to rescue Nicky from the snapping jaws.

Was he up to it?

He hoped to God he was, but he was afraid he was just the loser he had always been. When push came to shove, Lorenzo was always the first one out the door, saving his own ass, ratting out his friends, lying, stealing, cheating, doing whatever he had to do, just like all the other smacked out whores. Had he changed?

Maybe. Maybe not. Maybe once a whore, always a whore.

Sweetann's tiny sobs slowed. He stroked her soft hair as she wiped her face on the pillowcase.

If they got out of this with their skins on—if he found out that he could actually do the right thing for a change, he might think about settling down, and he could do worse than having Sweetann and her son by his side. Maybe they'd even start a little one of their own.

If she'd have him.

And why would she? He was a loser.

No, he wasn't. Not any more. He was clean and sober and had a good job and was going to school to start a real career, and they could make a good life together as a family.

Lorenzo couldn't believe he was having those thoughts, but there they were.

He was old enough. She was old enough. He may not be the smartest brick on the skid, but he liked to think he had something to offer. It was time he settled down and became respectable.

And here was this woman, this wonderful woman, her warm hands and soft lips making him, along with all his dark, self-loathing thoughts, most welcome in her bed.

He turned his attention to her, his heart swelling with emotion as he kissed away her tears and looked steadily into her trusting eyes.

He could be worthy of that trust.

He wanted to be worthy.

He wanted that more than anything else.

This time when he made love to her, he spoke her name, he stroked her hair, he kissed her eyelids.

The suitcase never entered his mind.

When he woke up, Natalie was gone. So was the suitcase.

The sun was up and someone was pounding on the door.

# Chapter 10

Horseteeth opened the sliding door of the van and gave Nicky a shove. He crawled in as fast as he could and scooted toward the other side. The van smelled like gasoline. Charlotte swung a weak fist at him when he tried to shove her, and yelled "Leave me alone!"

"You keep your fucking voice down," he said to her with a snarl, "or you won't have to worry about much of anything."

Charlotte got in the van on her own and climbed over to Nicky.

The little guy jumped in after her and pulled zip ties out of his back pocket. "Put'cher hands behind your backs," he said.

"No," Charlotte said. "I'm not letting you tie me up like that."

"You're being a problem," Horseteeth said, low and mean. "I don't think you want to know how fast we deal with problems. We hate problems."

Nicky put his hands behind his back and turned so that the little dark guy could tie him up. "C'mon," he whispered to Charlotte. "Do it."

She did as she was told, but when he zipped them down tight, she yelled again. "Ow!"

"Shut the fuck up," Horseteeth said, "or I'll slap your face right off."

"It hurts," she whined. "You did it too tight. It's cutting me."

Next were pillowcases over their heads, but that wasn't so bad. It quieted Charlotte down, like when they used to put a cover over the parakeet cage at night. When they had a parakeet. Nicky heard the little guy get out, close the big sliding door and get back in on the driver's side. The two men didn't talk at all.

He leaned up against Charlotte, more to comfort her than to comfort himself. He tried to remember the sequence of turns and stops as they drove, but they drove for too long, and he couldn't keep it straight. Once he gave up on that, he spent his time going over his lines for the play.

The ride was long and uncomfortable. The metal floor of the van was cold, and his shoulders hurt.

Charlotte cried.

Slowly, Nicky realized that Charlotte wasn't going to get them out of this. She may be the adult in charge, but Charlotte had no survival skills. She was just a kid, not much older than he was. And a girl. A stupid girl. Nicky was smarter. He'd take care of Charlotte. He'd save them both.

The first thing he had to do was pretend he was stupid. If they didn't expect much from him, he'd have the advantage of surprise.

The advantage of surprise. That's what his mom always told him. When you're in a situation and your back is to the wall, do the unexpected.

Well, his back was too the wall now. Literally.

He closed his eyes and cuddled up next to Charlotte. He hoped they weren't going to ride like this all the way to LA.

# Chapter 11

Lovemaking sounds in the other room woke Natalie from a sleep as light and peaceful as a soft blanket of snowflakes. She wasn't sure she had even been asleep, but she knew she didn't want to wake up, she didn't want to get up, but her bladder was full and her mouth was furry and tasted like vomit. The more aware she became, the more she realized her stomach was upset. The more awake she became, the more miserable she got.

She tipped out of the squeaky, metal-framed hide-a-bed and stumbled into the bathroom. She flicked on the harsh lights which squeezed her brain until she shut her eyes against it, opening them again slowly, letting the light in bit by painful bit.

She'd slept in her clothes. Her makeup was raccooned around her eyes, her hair was a ratty tangle, and saliva or something had crusted along the side of her mouth all the way down her chin.

And if that weren't enough, she'd started her period. Blood had seeped through her panties and on through her linen slacks. Shit.

She pulled them down and sat on the toilet, as sick and miserable as sick and miserable could get.

She took off her panties, put them in the trash and made do with a wad of toilet paper as a makeshift Kotex, but her slacks were beyond repair. Her new beige linen slacks. She washed her face and ran her fingers through the snakes of moussed hair that stood out on the sides of her head like clown hair. Then she rinsed her mouth, turned out the light and went back out into the dark, pre-dawn room.

Sweetann and Lorenzo were getting louder, and while Natalie wanted to smile over it all, she didn't feel like smiling. She didn't feel like being happy for them. She wouldn't mind a wild fuck with Lorenzo herself, and she sure as shit didn't want him to see her looking like this. She had no comb, no lipstick, no perfume, no makeup, no toothbrush. She didn't even have her purse.

But the keys to the BMW were on the table and that black suitcase stood like the Space Odyssey's monolith in the center of the room.

She wanted to go home. Shower. Change clothes. She'd come back for the three of them. She'd be home and back before they even knew she had gone.

She closed her eyes and thought for a moment.

Why were they here, in this—what, cottage?—instead of at home? There had been a problem, right? But she couldn't quite put her finger on what it was. Whatever, she could slide home for just a minute, and nobody would be the wiser.

If she took the car, they couldn't leave without her.

If she took the suitcase, they *wouldn't* leave without her. Not that they would, but she knew she could trust herself to behave with the suitcase, and she wasn't sure about the others. Especially Lorenzo. Especially Lorenzo and Sweetann. They could just take off, the two of them together, with all that good dope and all that cash, and have one hell of a honeymoon, leaving Richard and Natalie to save their own skins.

She wouldn't put it past them, not for one second.

She'd pick up Richard's toothbrush and pack a small bag for each of them. Sweetann and Lorenzo could fend for themselves. She'd buy breakfast croissants for them all on the way back.

Her stomach gave a lurch at the thought of food.

And she'd know that the suitcase with all of its very interesting contents would be safe and kept intact.

She picked up the keys, slid the suitcase toward the door. She stopped for a moment to make sure that she couldn't think of any reason why she shouldn't do this. She wondered briefly about her decision-making abilities. Then she felt the wad of tissue in her crotch, it sounded like Lorenzo and Sweetann were reaching some kind of a conclusion in the other room, and she knew she had no choice.

She opened the door, hefted the suitcase and walked outside. The BMW was parked right in front of the cottage, which appeared to be next to the pool house on some very fancy grounds. Who had friends with money like this? Lorenzo?

She walked quickly, not seeing anybody, but not wanting

anyone to see the stain on her slacks just in case someone happened to be peering out a window somewhere.

Her hands trembled on the steering wheel. The gate opened automatically, and she was out on the street.

In a brief flash of common sense, she looked at the gate, and noticed the address. Oh hell, she knew where she was. Just a few miles from home.

That didn't make driving any easier. It was hard to concentrate.

She was scared to death of being pulled over by a cop, because she had a suitcase full of money and dope and she didn't have a driver's license or any identification at all. Her nose kept running and she didn't have a tissue. She changed lanes erratically, and every time she did that, she told herself to get control. A moment later, she did something else that would appear stupid to any official observer.

Well, she thought, if all those years and all that money spent in and on college had taught her anything, it was that a little hair of the dog helped.

She pulled into a gas station and while the guy gassed up the car, she hauled the suitcase out of the trunk and into the filthy women's room and snorted a little of that sparkling magic powder.

She felt better instantly.

She'd done too much of it the night before. She thought it was coke, she thought they'd search for that elusive cocaine high before they got too speedy, so she had snorted quite a quantity.

But this wasn't cocaine, oh no, this was some entirely different animal, something that put her low instead of high, something, she had to admit, she quite liked.

And as soon as that tiny little pile of dusty brown powder on the end of her key went up her nose, she felt calm and self-assured. The trembling stopped. The slice in the brick needed a fresh piece of scotch tape, but she sealed it as well as she could. She'd fix it at home.

She got back into the car, gave the guy a hundred dollar bill, slid down in her seat, put it in gear, and cruised back home without a single erratic move.

The house looked fine. The tree-lined street was exactly the same, quiet and peaceful. She opened the garage door with the remote, cruised up the drive and right into the familiar haven. She closed the garage door, popped the trunk, then squeezed in behind the car, finishing off the linen slacks, and hauled the suitcase out and into the house.

She left it sitting in the kitchen, went upstairs and took a long, steamy shower. Her thinking seemed to be slow and methodical, and everything she did went just right, slowly, confidently.

She took her time fixing her hair and applying makeup to eyelids that wouldn't quite open all the way. She looked tired. She threw her cosmetics into a travel case, then put on jeans and a silk blouse. She packed a small bag for Richard with similar clothes, and filled his toiletries kit. She included an extra shirt for Lorenzo, and looked in the guest room for Sweetann's suitcase, but it wasn't there. Natalie had no idea what Sweetann had done with it, but she didn't much care. They had money; Sweetann could buy herself some fresh panties.

She set the packed bags by the garage door in the kitchen, then dragged the black suitcase into the living room. She wanted to put fresh tape on the cut in the brick before any of that precious stuff leaked out. She couldn't have any of this stuff go to waste. It was too precious. It was like magic dust.

No wonder people paid so much money for it.

She opened the suitcase wide on the living room floor and stared at all that money. And all that dope.

She would be a fool to run around town with that much.

She got a white plastic garbage bag from the kitchen and dumped all the cash into it, pulling ten hundred-dollar bills from the last packet before tossing it inside. As a last thought, she threw in one fresh brick of heroin. They could sell five bricks. She'd like to keep one on hand, just for... you know, personal use. Then she hauled the heavy bag upstairs into the bathroom, stood up on the sink and with Herculean effort, opened the little trap door in the ceiling and shoved the bag up into the insulated crawlspace.

Insulation drifted down and she squinted her eyes against it, but finally she got the little square lid back in place. She dusted herself off, made sure there wasn't any pink fluff in her hair, then went back downstairs, sour sweat staining her fresh blouse, but she didn't feel well enough to make the effort to change again.

She found the cellophane tape in the kitchen drawer, and tired of the project, she went back to the suitcase. This seemed like a whole lot of work. A lot of work somebody else should be doing.

She pulled off a length of tape, but before she sealed up that hole...

She pulled the cover off a copy of *Town and Country* that was sitting on the coffee table. She stuck the corner into the powder and lifted it to her nose. With one strong sniff, it was gone. A moment later, the world was right again. She didn't even know she'd been feeling a little edgy until that calm came to replace it. Then she folded up the piece of magazine cover and filled it full of powder, then tried to fold it into a clever little envelope the way she'd seen Lorenzo do it. It didn't come out exactly right, her fingers were clumsy, but it would do. She slipped that into her purse.

Then she fixed the rip in the plastic and just as she lifted the two halves of the suitcase together, she saw a bulge in the side pocket. Nobody had seen it because that's where all the cash had been. But there was a bulge, and it moved when she lifted up the side of the suitcase.

She reached in and touched metal.

Gunmetal.

Normally, Natalie would have freaked out and jumped away from it, but for some reason, the cool smooth heaviness of it felt very attractive. Careful to keep her fingers away from the trigger, she brought the gun out of the pocket and looked at it.

A short-barreled revolver.

Her fingers moved over its black surface with reverence. It felt so heavy, so powerful. She felt her eyelids grow ever heavier as she slid her fingers across the cold metal, and wanted to touch it to her warm cheek.

She heard the crackle of glass behind her, but not expecting nor recognizing the sound, and slow to react, the men were in the living room before she turned around.

"Just give us the case," the tall one said. His voice was that of a teenager, but he wore a black ski mask, so she couldn't tell his age.

"We don't want any trouble," the other one said with an equally young voice.

"No," she said, heart racing, brain not keeping up.

The tall one stuck a foot out, snagged the open suitcase with his toe and drew it across the living room floor away from her. "Where's the money?"

"Huh?" Events were confusing and happening too fast for Natalie, who felt as if a layer of glass had pressed down on her awareness, her reactions, her understanding, her emotions.

He closed up the case, picked it up and said, "Let's go."

"No," she said. "That's mine."

"It's ours," the kid said, and without another thought, Natalie pointed the gun at him and pulled the trigger.

Red sprayed the wall behind him. He jerked back and dropped, blood pouring out through the ski mask onto the beige living room carpeting.

"Holy shit," the other one said, then took off, sliding on the broken glass, escaping out the kitchen door.

Natalie stood up, blinking, not believing. Her ears rang in booming waves from the gunshot. Her hand felt numb and tingly. Her nose itched.

Her heart pounded, and the adrenaline threatened to lift the glass that pressed down upon her. She knew, in the back of her mind, that if that happened, she'd be horrified.

So she pulled the tape back from that brick and took another snort.

Fortified with extreme passionlessness, she took the suitcase, put it by the garage door with their overnight bags. She closed the outside kitchen door, and noticed the broken window for the first time. Sweat poured from her, sticking her silk blouse to her back.

One by one, she laboriously loaded the two overnighters and black bag into the BMW's trunk, her energy waning. She got her purse, and the keys, and the thousand dollars, and leaving the kid where he lay, opened the garage door and drove out.

Richard would know how to deal with this situation. Sweetann might even know how to get blood out of beige carpeting.

She put the gun on the seat next to her, pulled a tissue from her purse and dabbed at her running nose. She couldn't remember the street number of the house where the others were, but remembered the street. She hoped she'd recognize the gate.

She drove very, very slowly.

# Chapter 12

Lorenzo opened his eyes, fully aware that someone was pounding on the door. He blinked once, jumped out of bed and pulled on his pants.

Richard was sitting up on the hide-a-bed, disoriented. He was still fully dressed and he looked like hell.

Then the knock came again on the door, and Richard croaked out, "Who is it?"

"Police," came the answer, and fear pumped Lorenzo's muscles full of action before he remembered what it was he had done to be afraid about.

Natalie was not in bed with Richard.

The black suitcase was no longer in the room.

"Where's Natalie?" he whispered.

Richard shrugged.

Lorenzo gestured to where the suitcase was the last time he'd seen it and Richard shrugged again.

Lorenzo opened the door and two men in suits stood there. They briefly flashed badges. One held up a folded piece of paper and said, "We have a warrant to search the premises."

"Let's see it," Lorenzo said, but the cop whisked it back into his suit coat pocket.

"Lorenzo?" one of the cops said.

Lorenzo looked closer at the cop who had recognized him. Damn. "Boingo?"

"Fuck, man, long time no see." The two shook hands.

"You're a cop now?"

The cop looked at his shoes. "Yeah," he said, but Lorenzo knew he was lying. Boingo was no cop. He was a hood. Always had been, always would be. Small time hood. They had no badges, and they had no search warrants. In fact, Boingo hadn't shaved and looked hung over.

"Wow."

"Yeah, listen, we're looking for a shipment of dope. Four people and a suitcase full of horse."

Lorenzo frowned at the guy. He held up his scarred

forearms. "Clean and sober six years," he said. "I've got no interest in dope."

"We're going to have to search."

Sweetann came out of the bedroom, looking tousled, sleep-puffy and quite adorable. "Honey?" she said.

"Police are looking for something," he said to her, held out his arm and she snuggled up next to him.

"What?" she said.

The cop looked at the three of them. "Who's this?"

"I'm sorry," Lorenzo said. "This is Sally, my fiancée, and this is our friend Bobby."

"Only three of you?"

They all nodded.

"We're going to have to search."

"Help yourself," Lorenzo said. "But you've got the wrong place. How'd you get in the gate, anyway?"

"Not everybody who crashes in Jack's guest house is as squeaky clean as you are, Lorenzo. Jack has always been very helpful."

Lorenzo knew how to exist in this maelstrom of lies. It was still second nature to him. Lying was as easy as making conversation. He hated that about himself. It was part of his past.

"Slept in your clothes last night, eh, Bobby?" the other cop said to Richard.

Richard swung his legs over the edge of the bed. "Drank too much last night." Shit, looked like lying came easy to everybody, Lorenzo thought. He just prayed that Natalie, wherever the hell she was, wouldn't come waltzing in with that suitcase.

Boingo went into the bedroom. Then he looked in the closets, and in the bathroom. "Where's your luggage?" he asked.

"Didn't bring any," Lorenzo said. "We went out partying last night and had too much to drink. So we crashed here at Jack's rather than drive on back home."

"Smart," Boingo said. "But I thought you were clean and *sober.*"

"*They* had too much to drink," Lorenzo said.

"So what, you couldn't drive?"

"I didn't want Bobby puking in the back seat of my car," Sweetann said. "Jeez."

"Yeah? What kind of car would that be?"

"White Ford," she said, hoping there would be a white Ford out on the street like there was on every other street in America. "It's out on the street. Want the keys?" Sweetann challenged.

"Pretty fucking coincidental, looking for stolen goods and finding my old friend Lorenzo instead. And innocent at that." Boingo lifted up Richard's blanket that had fallen halfway to the floor and bent over to look under the hide-a-bed.

Then he tipped up the edge of the hide-a-bed, making Richard stand up. Richard took quick strides to the bathroom and emptied his stomach into the toilet.

Lorenzo cringed.

"Okay, Lorenzo. Take care, huh?" Boingo said. He had a squinty look that Lorenzo had always hated, and hated even more, six years later. Somebody was on to them big time, to locate them at Jack's, when Jack wasn't even in the country.

"Yeah," Lorenzo said. They shook hands, and the two suits left.

"White Ford," Lorenzo said to Sweetann, and they grinned at each other. "Hope there's one on the street."

"There's one on every street," she said, leaning against the wall, one finger in her mouth. "How do you know that guy?"

"There's one of those on every street, too," Lorenzo said. "We used to do drugs together. If he's a cop, I'm a girl."

Sweetann smiled and moved in next to him. He put his arm around her shoulders.

"So he's working for The Cook?"

"Cookie's guys know about me. He must be working for the airport guys."

"Oh yeah," she said. "How did they find us?"

Lorenzo shrugged. "They're pretty amazing."

"Where's Natalie?" Sweetann asked. "And the suitcase?"

"Good question," Richard said from behind them.

As if on cue, a timid knock came to the door. Lorenzo disentangled himself from Sweetann and took the two steps to open it. Natalie stood there, Richard's gym bag at her feet.

She looked white and waxy. Fragile. Her eyes were very strange, unfocused and a little wild. Lorenzo took her arm and pulled her in, kicked the bag inside, too, then looked around outside. Nobody in sight. He closed the door and threw the dead bolt.

"I brought you clothes," she said to Richard, then sat on the edge of the bed. A moment later, she tipped over sideways onto the mattress and closed her eyes.

"You went to the house?" Lorenzo couldn't believe it.

"Had to," she said softly.

"Did anyone see you?"

Her head moved in a tiny nod.

"She must've passed those guys outside," Sweetann said. "They must have let her in the gate."

Lorenzo grabbed his head with both hands, squeezed his eyes shut and then opened them and studied his feet. "We need a plan," he said. Then, remembering something important, he said, "Natalie, where's the suitcase?"

"Trunk," she breathed.

"At least she didn't carry it in here."

"Those guys'll see the BMW outside," Sweetann said.

"Too late," Lorenzo said. "We probably lost it all." Sweetann moved back in to put her arms around his bare torso.

"I'm going to take a shower," Richard said and picked up his bag.

"Stain on the carpeting," Natalie whispered.

All three of them looked at the carpeting, then at each other.

Richard looked confused. He blinked, squinted, as if thinking hurt him. Then he picked up the gym bag his wife had thoughtfully packed for him, and went back into the bathroom.

## Chapter 13

Sweetann ran her fingers over Lorenzo's smooth back and watched him watch Natalie doze. She wanted to hear him say more about that fiancée stuff. She wanted him to tell her that everything was going to be all right. She wanted to hear that even though The Cook knew her name and knew Nicky's name, that Nicky was safely on the train with Patty and that everything they all said was just posturing bullshit.

She had to keep her mind occupied or she would go insane with worry.

She tickled his palm with her nails and then entwined their fingers and pulled him toward the bedroom. He followed easily. She closed the door and scratched her hands in the black sculpted lines of glossy hair that ran across his chest and in a fine line down his flat belly. He wrapped his long arms around her, but the worry had again sprouted and it was too late to try to suppress it.

"What are we going to do, Sweets?" he asked.

She took her time answering. "Well," she finally said, "if those guys took the suitcase, there's nothing to do but go home."

"Right," he said.

"It was a pretty great adventure," she said.

"Sure was." He kissed her deeply, then walked her backwards to the bed, and guided her fall onto it. "Best time I've had in a long time." He kissed her, and sucked on her lower lip.

"But if they *didn't* take the suitcase..."

His hand stopped, his mouth stopped.

Shit.

"Then we're still in a heap of trouble," he said. "And we need a plan."

"One of us should run down to the car to see what the story is," she said.

"I'll go. You get your shower after Richard, and I'll rinse off when I get back. We've got to be ready to move." He bounced off the bed, then looked down at her, came back for one more good lip suck, then pulled her up with him. He opened the bedroom door and pounded on the bathroom door. "Richard. Come on!" He looked at Sweetann, kissed the top of her head. "Be right back," he said.

Sweetann sat on the edge of the hide-a-bed next to Natalie. Natalie's lids parted and she rolled her eyes around, found Sweetann, then closed again. "Natalie, you loaded?"

Natalie nodded. "Didn't mean to," she said.

"I'm in love."

Natalie nodded again.

"I mean it. Nicky's going to love him, too."

Natalie nodded again.

"I might move down here."

Natalie sighed.

"Well, maybe he'll move to Seattle."

Natalie made a little noise.

"People have done stranger things for love," Sweetann said to herself, because Natalie wasn't listening. Sweetann didn't know that she'd do just about anything for love, but she thought she might do just about anything for Lorenzo.

Richard came out of the steamy bathroom, clean shaven and smelling like cologne, with a towel wrapped around his waist. "Next," he said, and Sweetann took advantage of it.

The hot stinging water felt wonderful, and she soaped up and lathered her hair with somebody's leftover shampoo and just as her face was covered with suds, she felt a breeze, and within minutes, warm, soapy hands were massaging her breasts. She liked that. She wished for her razor, and her blow dryer, but hey, these were desperate times.

"Good news and bad news," Lorenzo said in her ear.

She turned and rubbed her soapy breasts against his chest while she soaped up his growing penis.

"The suitcase is there, but the money is gone."

"Natalie must have taken it," Sweetann said.

"Yeah, God, just don't stop doing that," Lorenzo said as she soaped up his scrotum, running her nails lightly over the tender skin and the tiny puckered area behind.

Sweetann immediately stopped what she was doing. The dope was still there; they had things to do. Nicky was on a train. She hoped to God Nicky was on a train.

She had to believe Nicky was on a train. She couldn't believe anything else. She *wouldn't* believe anything else.

She gave Lorenzo a shower-water kiss, rinsed off and stepped out.

Within minutes, the four of them were sitting around the coffee table, ready to make plans. Richard looked ill; he'd had a hard time putting the hide-a-bed back together; Lorenzo had to do it for him. Natalie sat next to him on the reconstituted couch, she was awake, but heavy-lidded.

Lorenzo sat in an overstuffed chair, too handsome with his twenty-four hour shadow, and Sweetann sat in another, a wheeled dining room chair, her feet on the coffee table, wheeling back and forth, back and forth. She toyed with her wet hair and hoped that this would be one of those miracle days when her hair dried attractively by itself.

"We could just go home," Richard said, "and tell everybody that Bongo or whatever his name was—the airport guys—got the dope and that's the end of the story. Then the big guys would think Bongo ripped them off, they'd kill him and everybody would be happy."

"Boingo," Lorenzo said, "not Bongo, and it's an idea."

"It's not a bad one," Sweetann said. "We could stash the dope somewhere, wait a year or so, *then* sell it."

Everybody looked at Natalie, and they knew that she couldn't be trusted to stay away from the dope or keep her mouth closed about it.

"What?" Natalie asked defensively, then crossed her arms in front of her chest and closed her eyes.

Sweetann opened her mouth to say something about waiting a year when Natalie slid into animation.

"I shot someone," she said quietly. Then in a burst of energy, she flung her arms out in a convulsive move, hitting Richard squarely in the chest. Her mouth hung open in an agonized mask and she reached for him and clutched at him, cords standing out in her neck. "My God," she said.

Richard clearly didn't know whether to hug her or get away from her.

"I killed someone," she said.

"What?" Disbelief was all over Richard's face, and Sweetann wanted to see if it was on Lorenzo's too, but she couldn't risk a glance for fear of missing something.

"At the house," Natalie started to cry, a high-pitched screamish cry. "A kid in a ski mask. He wanted the suitcase. I shot him."

"What?" Richard couldn't comprehend.

"Oh, God," she said, then fell over, her head in his lap, and sobbed.

Richard held his arms up, unwilling or unable to touch her. He looked to them for support, assistance, advice.

"Shot him with what?" Lorenzo asked.

Richard shook her shoulder and repeated the question.

"There was a gun in the suitcase," she squeaked out, then sat up, hiccing, looking like nothing Sweetann had ever seen before. She looked like a dragged down hooker, with her messed hair and her haunted eyes and her puffed lips. Sweetann went to the bathroom and came back with a handful of tissues.

"You shot somebody?" Richard was still wrapped around that nail of disbelief.

"He made a stain on the carpet," Natalie said. She blew her nose again and looked up at Sweetann. "Think it'll ever come out?"

Sweetann couldn't believe the question. She was already having a hard time believing her sister-in-law was snorting heroin, much less shooting people, crying about it for thirty seconds and then worrying about her interior decorating. It was all just a little too much. "Wait a minute," she said, and everybody looked at her. She held up her hands and closed her eyes. "I'm having a hard time with all of this. I can't believe this is happening to us."

"Well," Lorenzo said, "believe it. We're in deep."

"Nicky'll be here tomorrow night."

"It'll all be resolved before then," Lorenzo said, and reached over to take her hand. "One way or another."

"Police," Sweetann said. "Let's take the whole shootin' match to the police, confess any sins we've committed and get on about our lives."

"The airport guys will kill us all and put our heads on

stakes as a warning," Lorenzo said.

"Then let's kill them first," Natalie said, having no idea at all who she was talking about.

Sweetann couldn't imagine this new bloodlust coming from Natalie, but what she said made a sick sort of sense. "How about this? We sell the stuff in the suitcase to the Cook guy and get him to help us. We call the police on the airport guys and we don't tell anybody about the cash."

Lorenzo chewed on that for a while. "Could use some refinement, but I think it might work. Priority One is to save our own asses at this point, and the cash and the dope will have to go wherever it goes."

The room fell silent. Natalie was dabbing at her eyes and nose and looking at the tissue as if she expected to see something alien there. Richard stared straight ahead as if in some trance. Lorenzo sat perfectly still with his eyes closed, as if in prayer. Sweetann studied his beautiful profile, and felt overwhelming affection blossoming.

"Okay," he said, opening his eyes, the firm resolve of a plan clearly visible in them. "Richard. I'm going to take you and the ladies to a hotel. There's a Best Western not far from here. Then the three of you just sit tight. I'm going to take the Beamer back and pick up my bike. Then I'll start working the angles."

Richard nodded. Natalie nodded.

Sweetann shook her head, smiling apologetically. "I go where you go."

"I was hoping you'd say that," he said without smiling. "But realistically, it isn't possible. You might get hurt. I might get shot."

"We're in this together." She meant it. She meant it for this and every other adventure afterwards, for ever and ever 'til death do us part, amen. He probably didn't mean that, but she did. "Forget the bike. We'll rent a car."

"Okay," Lorenzo said. "Let's move."

~ ~ ~

They dropped a sickly looking Richard and a wasted Natalie at the motel. Lorenzo rolled down the window and gave them one last word. "We'll call you. If we haven't called by tomorrow morning, then you do whatever you want, because we'll be out of the picture."

Richard nodded.

Sweetann felt that high school naughtiness again, soaring on that unreal feeling of excitement and invincibility. It sounded so dramatic. Could it really be that dramatic? That dangerous? How could something this fun be so bad? She was cruising in a cool car with a cool guy and life couldn't be bad at all.

A dark cloud floated past her sun.

Nicky.

He was safe. With Patty. On a train.

But still her guts churned. She should never have left him. She should never have started this crazy thing. She should have just taken the wrong suitcase back and gotten hers and had a normal weekend.

If something happened to Nicky, she'd live with that for the rest of her life.

It was too much.

"Ready?" he said.

Afraid the weak sound of her own voice would start a whole new batch of tears, she looked out the side window and nodded.

Lorenzo put the car into gear and they headed back into the fray.

The gun was still wedged between the car seats. Lorenzo picked it up, disengaged the cylinder. Four bullets, one blank casing. He smelled it, then looked at Sweetann.

"You're kidding, right?" she said. Reality slapped her. She was going to get whiplash from the back and forth emotions.

"Smell this," Lorenzo said, and put the gun to her nose. It smelled like firecrackers. He snapped it closed.

"What are we going to do?"

"I owe somebody, Sweets. He's going to help us out of this and we're going to split the take with him."

Sweetann nodded. She wasn't greedy. Her mind had begun to drift toward Nicky and his train adventure. She thought that right now, nothing could possibly feel as good as a hug from that sweet ten-year-old boy.

They drove in relative silence back to town. Lorenzo pulled up in front of a rental car company, then turned to Sweetann.

"Do you have any cash?"

She shook her head. "Credit cards."

"They'd be on to us in a heartbeat with a credit card. We might as well keep the Beamer."

"They'd trace my credit cards?"

"Don't underestimate these folks, Sweets."

Sweetann remembered how The Cook knew her name and all about Nicky and Richard and Natalie within...within minutes.

"Then they might know that Nicky's on the train," she said, feeling out of breath. A claustrophobic feeling began to creep up over her skin, and she tasted something acidic, something awful at the back of her tongue.

She looked up and into the deep blue of Lorenzo's eyes. For all Lorenzo had been and done, there was still a depth of innocence in those eyes, a wide-open trusting that Sweetann could die for.

Could die for.

Might die for.

He smiled, a concerned, painful smile, and the corners of those fabulous eyes crinkled up. "It's a mess," he said. "But we're going to get out of it okay."

"I trust you."

"You fool." He smiled again and the creepiness receded. For the time being, at least. She had a feeling it would be back.

He started the car again and they drove up to a block of apartments. Lorenzo stuck the gun in his belt and said, "Stay here."

"Give it up," she said, and got out of the car with him.

They jogged across the street, eyes open, antennae waving, all senses on hyper alert.

Lorenzo lived on the first floor, apartment 108. The door was not locked.

He pulled the gun out and went in cautiously. Sweetann followed, her heart pounding so hard she could feel it pushing the backs of her eyeballs. In one sense, she felt like she was playing the part of a bad actress in a bad television series. In another sense, she felt like she could die at any moment.

He locked the door behind them. "It's been searched, but

not tossed," Lorenzo said. "That was decent of them." He relaxed, tucked the gun back into his waistband.

Sweetann took a deep breath.

He pressed the flashing button on the telephone answering machine, it beeped, and then Nicky's voice came into the room. "Mom?"

Sweetann's heart seized up and panic threatened weakened her legs. She almost fell to her knees.

Lorenzo held her up with a strong arm.

"Mom, Charlotte and I are here with William. We're okay, and he says not to worry. They have video games and a swimming pool. Charlotte's scared, but I—" Beep.

"Play it again," she said, desperate to listen to her baby's voice. They listened to it again. "He's okay, isn't he? He didn't sound hurt or scared or anything, did he?" She searched Lorenzo's face for signs of reassurance, for signs of doubt, for signs of precognition. She needed to be reassured so badly her chest hurt.

Lorenzo pulled her close to him and held her as her mind went around and around.

"Stop this, Lorenzo. I want this to stop. Right now. Give the money and the drugs to whoever. I don't care."

"Okay," he said. "Take a deep breath."

She wanted to scream, to claw at him, to punch, hit, gouge out her own eyes. Instead, she did as she was told. Took a breath. And another. And another, as deep as she could breathe, with Lorenzo holding her so tightly. A sort of calm returned to her and she knew Lorenzo was on her side. Natalie and Richard might be the enemy, but Lorenzo was not, and he'd help get Nicky back.

"They don't want him," Lorenzo whispered, his lips next to her ear. "They want the dope."

The phone rang and they both jumped.

It rang again and with one arm around Sweetann, Lorenzo picked up the receiver, but held it wide so Sweetann could hear the conversation.

"Hello?"

"Hello, Lorenzo."

"Cookie."

"That was a stupid move, Lorenzo. I'm giving you one chance to make it good."

"They've got Sweetann's kid."

"I know. You help me put those thugs out of business, I'll get the kid back."

Sweetann felt Lorenzo's muscles tighten. He put the phone closely to his ear and turned away from her.

"You've never been known for your compassion or your altruism, Cookie."

"Hey, I got kids. I know about kids. I'm not cold. But I'm talking business, Lorenzo. You let my first offer expire on the goods, and now we're talking a different offer. No money, just the kid. You give me the stuff—hell, you can keep the cash—just give me the powder and I'll get you the kid."

"They said the same thing."

"You and I have history, Lorenzo. Help me put those assholes away."

"Call me back in five," Lorenzo said, and put the phone down. He walked Sweetann to the living room where they sat in the two rickety lawn chairs that made up the entirety of his decor.

"Let's do it!" Sweetann said, clutching his jacket when he told her what The Cook had said.

"Not so fast," Lorenzo countered, prying her fingers loose. "He can make all kinds of promises and then forget them all and slink back under the rock he came from. We've got to protect ourselves."

Sweetann wondered if Lorenzo had lost his mind. "Protect ourselves? What about Nicky? Who knows what they're doing to him? Protect *ourselves*? We have to protect *him*!"

"Sweetann, honey, settle down a little bit. We're not going to save Nicky if we fuck this up. Now listen to me. Are you listening to me?"

Sweetann pulled her cell phone out of her purse and turned it on. One message from Patty. She dialed the retrieval number.

"Sweetann, it's Patty. I'm at your place, and Nicky and Charlotte aren't here. The front door was unlocked. I don't know what to do. Should I be calling the police? Are you in trouble? Call me."

Sweetann found it hard to breathe.

Deep breath, she told herself. And another.

She had to jangle for a few moments before she could settle down. Patty had been too late. Nicky was not on a train with her best friend. Instead, he and Charlotte had been kidnapped by the airport drug runners.

Kidnapped.

"Sweets?" Lorenzo took the phone from her, hit 3 to replay the message.

Their eyes locked as he listened to Patty's voice.

Sweetann's mind cleared in a strange way, and things went into slow motion. All the options were laid out in logical order. She had to be the adult in charge. It was her son who was in jeopardy, nobody else's. Nobody cared about it the way she did, it was up to her to save him, no matter who had to be sacrificed in the process. She was the one who got Nicky into this mess, she had to be the one to get him out.

Freaking out and being hysterical was not going to do anything to save her boy. She had to be cool. She had to play her cards right. She had to do whatever it took.

*Whatever it took.*

Then she took a deep breath, sent an abstract prayer out into the ether, consciously relaxed her shoulders and looked into the pure blue of Lorenzo's caring eyes.

"If you're going to go off the deep end, I'm going to stash you someplace and take care of this myself," he said.

"No," she said, then took another deep breath. "That won't be necessary."

"I won't hesitate."

Sweetann knew this was not an empty threat. "I'm okay. I have to hold it together or Nick won't have a chance."

"That's right." His look softened. She saw admiration in his eyes. He leaned forward and kissed her on the forehead. "You know, if we get out of this in fairly good shape—"

Sweetann was hearing words she had longed to hear for the past nine years, but she was in no mood to hear them now. She waved him off. "I can't listen to that now. I need to hear your plan. Get on with it, because I need to call Patty and tell her why she can't find—" panic stole her voice. She gasped, choked, and then regained her backbone. "Why Nicky isn't home."

Lorenzo nodded and handed her the phone.

# Chapter 14

When Nicky woke up, the first thing he noticed was the smell in the room. He wasn't at home. This place smelled like dogs and cigarettes. He sat up, rubbing his face, and then he remembered that William guy coming to get him in the night, making him get dressed, and Charlotte, too, and then bringing them to this house in that rusty old van.

It had been like a bad dream, but he smelled stinky dog and knew that something weird was happening. This wasn't at all right.

He wanted his mom.

He got out of the twin bed, went over to the door and tried the knob. Locked. He figured as much. It was just like in the movies.

He'd been kidnapped. Him and Charlotte.

Why?

Red marks still ringed his wrists from the zip ties, but it wasn't too bad. He wanted to be afraid, but sat up straight instead. He had to be smart, not scared. His mom would be scared enough for all three of them.

He couldn't afford to be afraid. He had to be smart and act dumb and not be afraid. It probably wasn't going to take too much to act dumber and be smarter than Horseteeth. Or William, as he wanted to be called.

The bedroom he was in was bare, with nothing on the walls. There was a small television on the dresser, a box of old videogames next to it, and that was about it. The carpet was brown and probably full of dog hair. An old blanket was on the bed with some dingy sheets and a dingier pillow.

He pulled open the draperies, stood on the bed and looked out the window. Fenced yard. Regular neighborhood. They were in somebody's house. He needed to pee.

He went back to the door and knocked on it. "Somebody?" he called. "I need to go to the bathroom."

He heard scuffling sounds in the next room, and soon the door opened, and it was William, with a cigarette in the corner of his mouth. He'd pulled his scraggly hair back into a pitiful little pony tail. He opened the door wide, and pointed at the bathroom down the hall. "Be quick," he said. Nicky went in there and closed the door.

He didn't feel scared, exactly, but he didn't know what he should feel. It didn't seem like they were going to hurt him, or they already would have. Instead, they gave him a television set with some stupid old video games, but that was better than being handcuffed or blindfolded or something.

He wondered where Charlotte was. He wondered what this was all about. It couldn't be about money. He and his mom didn't have any. Charlotte sure didn't have any, and neither did her parents.

It was something else. He had a feeling that if he could figure out what that something else was, he'd have an idea on how to get out of it.

When he had washed his hands, he opened the bathroom door, and William was standing there, gesturing for him to go back into the bedroom. "Where's Charlotte?" he asked.

"Nicky!" He heard her call out to him from behind the closed door across the hall. Probably another stinky bedroom.

"In here," William said, and gave Nick a shove into the room. "Behave yourself. We're going to leave in a little while."

"Where are we going?"

"To LA," William said, then closed the door.

"To see my mom?" No answer. He pounded on the door. "Hey, are we going to see my mom?" Still no answer.

Nick had no idea what was going on. He could climb up on the bed, open the window and climb out, but why would he do that if William was going to take him to see his mom? Something wasn't right, but if Nick behaved himself, things would work out okay. They always did. His mom said that they always did. And they always had. He didn't know where he was or what he'd do if he climbed out of the house and left Charlotte, who probably wouldn't even think of climbing out the window.

Charlotte was still yelling his name, and then he heard her bedroom door open and close. That gave him a dark feeling. He sat on the edge of the bed, guts in a knot, worried about

Charlotte. He was worried about a lot of things, but he mostly worried about his mom.

She was in trouble and he wasn't there to protect her. Uncle Richard and Aunt Natalie were going to be no help, whatever it was. He would never want to have to count on them, and he knew that his mom couldn't count on them, either. Aunt Natalie drank too much and Uncle Richard never knew what to say to him. He always just patted Nicky on the head like a dog and asked him how school was and if he had a girlfriend yet. Stupid.

Hey, speaking of a dog, there was a dog somewhere in this house. Playing with a dog would be a lot more fun than those old video games.

Nicky got up off the bed and started pounding on the door again. "Hey! Where's the dog? Let me see the dog!"

But he got no response. Eventually, he gave up and lay back down on the bed.

If he was writing this play, what would happen next? His mom, Charlotte, Horseteeth, the little guy...

He hated every conclusion he thought of.

But actors had power to interpret the play. Maybe he couldn't influence all the other actors in this play, but he might be able to do something about the ending.

He visualized a happy ending, standing next to his mom, her warm hand on his back.

# Chapter 15

"Should we call the police?" Natalie asked as she put her bag down on the tired bed in the worn out Best Western. Natalie had never stayed in such a dump, and felt distaste rising all around her. She didn't want to touch anything. It all looked germ-infested.

"Police?" Richard asked. He kept moving around, looking in the shower, in the closets, in the drawers. He was making Natalie nervous.

"Yeah, about...you know, about the kid...I...shot."

"Not yet. Let's wait to hear from Lorenzo first." Richard sat on the edge of the bed. "You really shot him? Maybe you just wounded him or something."

Natalie chewed on a fingernail. They were acrylic, and not very satisfying to chew. She hadn't chewed a fingernail since college finals, but she was chewing them now. "Yeah, maybe."

Richard sat down on the bed for a brief moment, then stood up and began to pace. "I can't just sit here and wait for them to call."

"What else?"

"I don't know. But this doesn't seem right, them roaming around in our car with all that money and all that... money."

"They don't have the money."

Richard raised an eyebrow. "You got the money?"

Natalie nodded, inspecting her damaged fingernail. She could leave Richard here and go find a nail place to have it repaired. That would be good, productive use of their waiting time.

"Where is it?"

"I'm not telling," she said.

"At the house?"

"The fewer people who know, the better." Richard was the last person she was going to tell. She had just this second decided that the money was going to buy her way out of this marriage. Richard had no idea, of course, but he probably wouldn't squeal too loudly when she just took off and never came back. He could go spend the rest of his days with his Latin whore. He didn't think she knew, but of course she did. A wife always knows.

He never wanted to have a baby with her.

Shit. She didn't want to have a baby with him, either. He was a loser.

She examined that fingernail again. Hmmm. Maybe when she went to get her nails done. She'd just swing by the house, grab the loot and never look back. The thought made her smile, even though she didn't have the energy for any of that. The plan sounded good, but she didn't have anything of what it would take to pull it off. Not yet anyway.

Richard lifted himself off the bed and went into the bathroom. Then he came back and resumed pacing.

"Settle down, willya?" she said.

"I don't like being out of the loop. When you're out of the loop, you're out of control. You're out of it."

Natalie fetched her purse and pulled out the little envelope. "Here. This'll settle you down a little bit."

"That stuff'll make a junkie out of you," Richard said.

He didn't understand. Desperate times called for desperate measures. If she was going to sit in this crappy hotel room for a whole goddamned day while Sweetann and Lorenzo fucked themselves into a state of oblivion, she was going to enjoy her own little taste of nirvana.

She tipped a little onto the nightstand and then snorted it. She felt better immediately. "Want some?" she asked.

"No."

"Okay." She left the paper where it was, and laid back on the bed, which was not so bad after all.

Maybe she'd set her eyelid dreams on her new life without Richard, a life with lots of money to spend however she wanted.

Sweet, sweet dreams.

# Chapter 16

Richard watched Natalie put more of that powder up her nose, and the last wisp of affection for her slipped away.

She had a huge wad of hundred dollar bills at her elbow and a pile of heroin sitting inside the crinkles of a magazine cover.

How could he ever imagine her to be the mother of his children?

Ludicrous.

He watched her toot up and whack out, his feelings for her flickering like bad television reception. Hard to believe he'd ever thought he could make a mother out of her. Booze had always been Natalie's master, and now she'd traded that in for something infinitely more destructive. She liked it that way. The more destructive, the better. The faster the ride to hell, the more attractive it was to her.

He shook his head, shuffled his feet, flopped down into an uncomfortable little motel chair. He wouldn't make that mistake again. He'd get his share of the money—call it compensation for time and energy spent with Natalie and her petty ways—and then he'd be gone. Long gone.

He reached into the coffee table drawer and pulled out the phone book. He turned to the Travel Agents. It was Sunday and they wouldn't be open, so he just slid down in the chair, rested his head on the back, the phone book open in his lap, and daydreamed about where he would spend his retirement and his share of that money.

Lorenzo didn't have exclusive rights to the Big Score dream.

Within moments, Richard was asleep, dreaming of bad guys with no faces chasing him around and around a tropical island. He was barefoot, running in sand, and had some kind of irritating strings or something dangling from the back of his jacket but he couldn't reach them, because his hands were full, carrying his dope and cash in canvas bags with big dollar signs painted on them.

# Chapter 17

Lorenzo pulled the BMW up to the seedy bar and parked where they had parked just the evening before. Twelve hours that felt like twelve lifetimes had passed. The bar and the neighborhood had seemed spooky and menacing at night, and daylight did nothing to ameliorate that image.

They both jumped out of the car, Lorenzo took Sweetann's hand, and they pushed open the big door and entered the smoky, moldy, dark, damp and stinking interior.

Sweetann thought she had entered the Twilight Zone. She could swear it was the same bartender and the same guys playing pool. And for certain, there was the same steady stream of smoke coming up from the back booth. It was like that guy never smoked the cigarettes, he just lit them, took the initial drag and then just let them smolder.

Lorenzo pulled her straight back to the corner, where she met the owner of the cigarette smoke.

Charles looked like he had been sculpted into the booth. He looked like he had never seen the light of day. Pale, thin, yellow and wrinkled, he probably stumbled onto some stained blue-ticking mattress in the back room of this bar for an hour or two of sleep once or twice a day. Then he dressed back in the same shiny brown suit he'd worn every day for the past thirty years and resumed his vigil in this stupid booth in this nasty place. Never showering, never eating, just smoking and reading.

What was he doing? Waiting for something to happen? Waiting to die?

This could be my father, she thought, my grandfather. This guy had made a wrong turn somewhere and this was what he ended up with.

She'd have to tell Nicky about this guy. Make certain he didn't make a similar wrong turn.

Words she'd do well to heed her own damn self, as she was making a whole series of wrong turns.

Sweetann knew this was a bad guy, knew he was a drug

runner, or that he worked for some criminal organization, but looking at him, at his watery eyes and his expressionless face, her emotions seized her again. This had been somebody's precious little ten-year-old boy at one time. What the hell happened? She wanted to like him. She wanted to do nice things for him. He ignited her mothering instincts. She wanted to improve his life. She wanted to make him smile. She wanted to steam him up a big bowl of vegetables. He looked like he hadn't eaten a vegetable in a decade or more.

But he did smile. Charles gave Lorenzo a smile of genuine delight when he slid into the booth opposite him, and Sweetann slid in and touched her thigh to Lorenzo's.

"This is—"

"Sweetann Holt," Charles said, then extended a long, thin hand with yellow nicotined fingernails. Sweetann shook his hand, forcing a smile back at him, although she hated the fact that all these criminals knew her name.

Lorenzo put both his hands on the table and leaned in toward Charles. "I have an offer for you."

Charles waved him away. "Don't bother, Lorenzo, it's been tried before."

Lorenzo didn't even flinch. "It's not a huge sum of money, Charles, but it'll get you out of his fucking bar. You could move to Arizona or something. Sit by the pool and watch girls in bikinis."

"You think The Cook don't have Arizona?"

"Tahiti, then. Bali. Christ, Charles, I don't know. I just know that it makes me sick to think of you in here just...dying. You're dying in here, Charles."

"What's your offer?"

"One fifth for Sweetann's kid."

"You're going to burn the airport and slide under The Cook?" Charles smiled indulgently, as if he were talking to a child. He tipped his dead cigarette butt onto the mound of scorched filters just like it, slid a fresh cigarette from the pack on the table, lit it, inhaled deeply, then set it in the ashtray to burn down. "You've got huevos. And you want me to help you. I'm flattered."

Lorenzo sat back, sighed in frustration.

"You don't have to do anything," Sweetann piped up. "Just tell me how to get my little boy back."

"You know, Charles," Lorenzo said, leaning forward again, "The Cook isn't going to get the boy back, no matter what he says."

Charles nodded.

"And the airport guys don't care about him, either. Once they've got their stuff—"

Charles nodded again.

"You have kids, Charles?" Sweetann asked.

Charles nodded slowly. "Used to."

Sweetann pulled her wallet from her purse, opened it to a snapshot of Nicky in his little league uniform. His teeth gleamed white under a sunburned nose, his red-brimmed cap pulled down to shade his green eyes.

Charles didn't even look at it. "Don't lean on me," he said to her, and she pulled the photo back. "Sentimentality ain't my strong suit. If I help you it's because Lorenzo and I have a history. He's cleaned up real good and it would be nice to see him with a family." He looked at Lorenzo. "Not because of Arizona."

"Bikinis," Lorenzo said.

Charles laughed. Lorenzo laughed, Sweetann smiled, not quite getting the private joke.

Charles fixed his watery eyes on her. "Go get me a cup of coffee, will you, doll? Black."

Sweetann slid out of the booth, and when she came back with a steaming mug, Lorenzo was sliding out. She set the mug down in front of Charles.

"Thanks," he said.

"C'mon," Lorenzo said, grabbed her arm and hustled her out of the bar.

"What'd I miss?"

"Get in the car."

She stamped her foot, she slammed her hand on the top of the car. "Tell me."

"Get in the car."

"It's my kid."

"Keep your voice down. Just get in the goddamned car."

She got in, fuming.

"Relax," Lorenzo said. "Charles is an old man, he's used to doing things the old way and that doesn't include women."

"So?"

"So we're to take the stuff back to the zoo. Charles is going to find us a buyer, then he's going to find Nicky, and then he's going to meet us there."

This was all good news. She should have trusted Lorenzo's judgment all along. "I think I love you," Sweetann said, the statement taking both of them by surprise.

He paused for a moment, staring straight ahead. Sweetann winced at her impulsive statement, but Lorenzo turned toward her, affection in his eyes and in his touch when he grazed her cheek with a fingertip. "Then you win a Big Mac," he whispered, and started the car.

## Chapter 18

Surrounded by greasy paper, cardboard, Cokes, French fries, burgers and that horrible, oily, delicious smell, Lorenzo and Sweetann sat in the BMW and ate. They both leaned against their respective doors, facing each other, sharing two orders of fries that they'd dumped in the bottom of the takeout bag.

Sweetann was ravenous, and scarfed down the hamburger faster than she could have imagined. Lorenzo was into his third when she wadded up the paper and started to tidy up.

The food settled her belly, calmed her nerves, and she hadn't thought of Nicky for almost ten minutes. Now when she did, it wasn't with a rasping, painful, grinding fear, it was with anxiety and dedication to taking each step purposefully and sure-footedly, in order to get him back safely into her arms.

Sweetann checked her teeth in the visor mirror, licked her fingers and wiped them off, then settled back, sipped her Coke and watched Lorenzo. "If Charles pulls this off," she said, "he can live with Nicky and me and I'll cook and care for him for the rest of his days."

Lorenzo shook his head no as he chewed and swallowed the last half of the burger and washed it down with a good eight ounces of Coke. When his mouth was empty, he wiped his lips on a napkin, burped gently and smiled at her. "You're going to be doing that for me," he said. "Besides. Charles needs to go to Arizona or someplace warm, not Seattle."

"You think we'll be living in Seattle?" Sweetann was happy to fall into that fantasy, at least for a moment.

Lorenzo settled back too, satisfaction on his face. Sweetann thought that was the finest sight imaginable.

"Where would you like to live?" he asked.

"Italy."

"Italy it is," he said. "Do you speak Italian?"

"Not yet."

"Well, we should stop and get a phrase book, because once we get Nicky, we might not want to dawdle in a bookstore."

That danger thing pressed back inside the car again. For a while it was gone, and Sweetann had a moment of feeling free. But it was back now, oppressive, dark and heavy. Sweetann straightened up in her seat and buckled her seat belt.

It was time to go.

Lorenzo did the same, tucked his Coke between his legs and started the car. "I think we ought to leave all this fast food paper and stuff for Natalie and Richard to clean up."

"Yeah," Sweetann said. "I think I'll even leave a couple of fries under the seat."

"That'll teach 'em to drive a BMW."

That should have been funny, and under other circumstances, it would have been.

~ ~ ~

The abandoned warehouse known as the zoo was locked. No cars on the cracked concrete that used to be its parking lot. Just an old, rusted truck up on blocks in the corner. Weeds grew from under its hood. Lorenzo and Sweetann sat in the car and waited.

"If we had cards, we could play gin," Lorenzo said. "Do you know how to play gin?"

"No."

"I'll teach you."

A black sedan pulled up and parked behind them.

"Timing is everything," Lorenzo said. He sat and waited.

"Should we go talk to them?" Sweetann asked.

"Let them come to us."

A tall, thin black man got out of the driver's seat, walked over to the warehouse door and keyed the lock. He went inside with no acknowledgement at all that they were sitting there, waiting.

Lorenzo looked in the rear view mirror, but couldn't tell if anybody else was in the sedan. They waited.

Soon the man came back out the warehouse door and stood, looking around, hands in his pockets, as if he had all the time in the world. Then he walked leisurely over to Sweetann's door.

Lorenzo turned the key and powered down the window.

"You got the airport bag?"

Sweetann nodded.

"Let's see it."

Lorenzo carried the suitcase into the warehouse and set it on a piece of plywood that spanned two sawhorses. He unzipped the top and flipped it open.

The man came over, perspiration shining his forehead.

"I count five. Charles said six."

Sweetann and Lorenzo looked at each other. "There are six," he said, then they looked in the bag, looked around in the bag, felt in the side pockets, as if they were big enough to conceal a brick of heroin. "There *were* six," he said.

"I want six or nothing," the man said, pulled a cell phone out of his pocket and punched in a number.

"Charles, you trying to bust my balls here?" He listened for a moment then handed the phone to Lorenzo.

"I don't know," Lorenzo said into the phone, and Sweetann saw the blood drain from his face.

"Natalie," she whispered at him. Understanding spread across Lorenzo's face.

"Hey, Charles, I know where the other one is. It's with the money. I'll go get it...Yeah, I know...Yeah, I'm sorry...Yeah." He handed the phone back to the man, who listened for a moment, then clicked the phone off.

"One hour," Lorenzo said.

"One hour could mean my ass."

"One hour." Lorenzo closed the suitcase and picked it up off the table.

The man looked at his watch. "You got fifty-nine minutes," he said. "I'll keep this here with me."

"No, I'll keep it with me," Lorenzo said, zipped it shut and picked it up. "You can have it when you can have it all. We'll be back in an hour."

"Fifty-nine minutes."

It was hard to leave without running, but they managed it. They erased half the street with tire rubber on their way to the Best Western, cursing Natalie all the way. Well, cursing Natalie half the way. The other half of the way, Lorenzo cursed himself for not checking the suitcase carefully enough, not following along behind Natalie.

He hoped to God that Natalie had the dope with her, because they'd be hard pressed to make it all the way out there and back again as it was. Another stop just might push Charles and his business partner over the line.

They pulled up under the port-cochére and jumped out of the car. Holding hands, they ran into the hotel lobby.

"Richard—" Lorenzo looked at Sweetann helplessly.

"Preston," Sweetann said. "Richard and Natalie Preston's room, please."

The desk clerk was clearly in no hurry. No hurry to iron his shirt, no hurry to comb his hair, and certainly no hurry to help these people who were not guests of his hotel. He walked in what seemed like slow motion to the card file. He looked, then looked again.

"I'm sorry," he grinned. "There's no one registered by that name."

"They used a different name," Sweetann said to Lorenzo. "Look," she said to the unkempt clerk, "they checked in this morning. Tall, nice looking guy—"

"Tall, tired blonde with him?" the clerk asked.

"Yes," Lorenzo said. "They probably paid in cash."

"With a one-hundred dollar bill," the clerk said.

"That's them."

"We don't give out room numbers."

Sweetann felt Lorenzo heat up beside her.

"Would you call their room, then, please, and let me talk with them?"

"Just a moment," the clerk said, and answered the buzzing telephone.

"He wants you to tip him," Sweetann whispered to Lorenzo.

Lorenzo fumbled in his pockets and came up with a ten-dollar bill.

The clerk began taking a reservation over the telephone and Lorenzo began to bounce up and down on his toes. When the clerk finally hung up, Lorenzo snapped the ten and put it on the counter. "Would you please ring their room?"

The clerk snatched the bill and smoothed down his hair. "Certainly. And you are?"

"Lorenzo."

"Lorenzo..."

"Pickles."

Sweetann looked at him in amazement. She'd never known Lorenzo's last name before. "Pickles?"

"Quiet," he said under his breath.

But she was beyond being quiet. All the tension, all the danger, all the hurry and worry and deadline and irritation paled in the hilarity of the moment. "Lorenzo Pickles?" she asked, quietly screaming it.

Even Lorenzo couldn't keep a straight face. "So?" he asked mock-defensively.

"Lorenzo PICKLES?"

"Yes, now shut up."

But she was out of control. Even the desk clerk stopped dialing mid-number in order to watch Sweetann laugh until the tears came down her cheeks. "Lorenzo and Sweetann Pickles," she gasped, and then Lorenzo began to laugh with her.

"Hey," Lorenzo said, completely forgetting the desk clerk and the ticking of the clock, "Pickles is a fine family name. I come from a long line..."

"Kosher?" she gasped out and even the desk clerk began to laugh.

In a moment, Sweetann regained control of herself, wiped her eyes and her nose, and stood next to him, trying to act normal. The desk clerk was still watching her with a smile on his face and the telephone in his hand.

"Please call," she said. "It's Lorenzo Pickles here to see the tall guy with the tired blonde. Oh, God." She retained control with great difficulty.

"It's my name," Lorenzo said with a quiet smile, "and I'm proud of it."

"Of course you are," she said, wiping her eyes.

"There's no answer," the desk clerk said.

All hilarity vanished.

"They're here," Lorenzo said. "What room number?"

The clerk fingered the ten without looking up at them.

"Oh, for Christ's sake." Lorenzo pulled out a twenty and laid it on the counter. "Give me back the ten."

The clerk took the twenty, folded it with the ten and put it in his pocket. "208."

"Give us a key," Sweetann said.

The clerk patted his pocket, the one with the cash.

"Don't fuck with me," Sweetann said. "That's my sister and she might be in trouble."

Something in her tone, or the fact that she was the tired blonde's sister, or the idea that that blonde could easily be in trouble, the way she looked, or perhaps it was because he liked this spunky woman who could laugh with such abandon, or because he realized that she could marry this guy and become Sweet Pickles and could use a break—something made the desk clerk pull out an extra key and hand it to her.

"Thanks," she said, grabbed Lorenzo's hand and they ran outside, around the corner and up the stairs.

No one answered the knock, so Sweetann put the key in and turned it.

Natalie was asleep. Richard was not in the room.

"Natalie?" Sweetann went over to her, but Natalie wasn't sleeping, she was unconscious. Sweetann saw the pile of heroin on the desk.

"Lorenzo," she said, panic rising, afraid she was about to lose her entire family over a stupid misdirected suitcase, "help me."

"Go through their bags," Lorenzo said, nodding toward Natalie and Richard's overnight bags which were stashed in the closet on the floor.

Lorenzo sat on the bed next to Natalie. She looked pale and flaccid, a look he had seen on hundreds of druggies before. The look frightened him. It was a universal truth, that look, and he had barely escaped it.

He picked up her limp shoulders and brought her to a sitting position. "Natalie?" he said, gently shaking her.

Her eyes fluttered.

"Sweetann, honey, bring me a cold washcloth." He returned to Natalie, shaking her gently again. "Natalie, come back to us."

Her eyelids opened, her eyes rolled. They focused in on Lorenzo, then went away. He shook her again, not hard, just enough to get her attention. She frowned in annoyance.

"Where's the brick?" he asked her.

She smiled, a vague, vacant smile.

Sweetann handed him a washcloth. "It's not here," she said. "Natalie, goddammit, *wake up!*"

Natalie's eyes came open again, focusing first on Lorenzo, then on Sweetann.

"Where's the brick?" Lorenzo asked again.

"Home," she said.

Lorenzo looked at his watch. "Fuck." Then, back to Natalie. "Where's Richard?"

Natalie shrugged, then struggled weakly until Lorenzo let her lie down again. Her head dropped sideways into the crack between the pillows, and she didn't look comfortable, but they left her that way, her eyes closed.

"Flush that shit," he said, and just as Sweetann scooped it up off the desk, the door opened and the desk clerk stuck his head in.

"Everything okay in here?"

"Yeah," Lorenzo said. "Natalie is sick."

"Should I call an ambulance?"

"No, she'll be all right. Her husband will be back soon."

"I don't want nobody dying on my shift."

"There's no problem," Lorenzo said.

Sweetann came out of the bathroom with a freshly moistened towel and made a big show of putting it on Natalie's forehead. That comforted the desk clerk.

"Okay, then," he said, backed out and closed the door.

"We can't wait for Richard," Lorenzo said.

"How can I leave her like this?" Sweetann said.

They looked at each other for a long moment, neither wanting to leave the other.

Sweetann looked down at Natalie, whose mouth was open in a pose that would horrify her under normal circumstances. For a moment, Sweetann wished she had a camera for blackmailing purposes. She felt the family tug, the pull of guilt, the hopelessness of loving such a stupid bitch as Natalie, but she also felt the overwhelming urge to go toward the light, the love, the future, with Lorenzo.

*Nicky.*

Natalie really wasn't Sweetann's problem. She was Richard's problem. Sweetann had the future to think about, and the future was Nicky.

"Think she'll be all right?" Sweetann finally asked.

Lorenzo nodded. "She'll sleep it off."

"Okay, then." Sweetann moved a pillow under Natalie's head, closed her mouth, folded the damp towel and left it on her forehead. Then with one guilt-ridden backward glance, she let Lorenzo hustle her out the door.

~ ~ ~

With barely ten minutes before Charles's offer expired, Lorenzo and Sweetann cruised quietly down the street in front of Richard and Natalie's enormous brick house. The beige McMansion looked quiet. It looked normal. Sweetann wondered if Richard had hit their parents up for the money to build it and then conveniently lost the paperwork when they died. That would answer a lot of questions.

Lorenzo drove by, went down a few blocks, stopped under a huge shade elm and looked at each other.

"There's a dead guy in the living room," Sweetann said. "Hard to believe."

Lorenzo took the fast food bag full of unwanted onions and cold, dead fries wadded up in orange wax paper and handed it to Sweetann. "Okay," he said. "I've got a plan." He turned the car around, drove quietly down the calm street and parked in front of the house, right behind his Harley. "Quickly, Sweets. We go in, we get out. We've got nine minutes to find the brick and get it back to the zoo."

She opened the car door, then felt his cool hand on the back of her neck.

"Kiss me for luck," he said.

She did, although it wasn't much of a kiss. Even her lips were tense.

Instead of going through the garage, they walked up to the front door and opened it with a key that was on the BMW's key ring.

The blood on the wall was the first thing Sweetann saw. It stunned her to immobility. Lorenzo pushed her into the room and pulled the door shut behind him. "When we're finished, we'll call the cops," he whispered. "Quickly, now."

He pulled her through the too-quiet, spooky house and up the stairs. She went into Natalie and Richard's opulent bedroom and began searching. Lorenzo went into the guest room, started ransacking the closets.

"Faster, Sweets," he said, poking his head in the door. "I'm going to the basement."

Sweetann nodded, then continued her work, distasteful as it was, going through all Natalie's drawers. She knew she ought to just toss the stuff, but she couldn't bring herself to mess up this professionally kept room. She worked with urgency, but her bladder and that big Coke was working on her with equal urgency. When she couldn't stand it another minute, she ran to the bathroom, pulled down her jeans and with a sigh, let it go.

There was pink fluffy dust on top of the toilet paper roll. There was more on the counter top, more in the sink.

She looked up.

The attic.

She flushed the toilet, closed it and stood on the seat, then stepped up to the counter top, moved the crawlspace lid aside. The plastic bag of money almost came down and hit her on the head. Pink insulation showered down on her and she squinted in time, but still got a mouthful.

"Four min—" Lorenzo said, saw what she was doing, and ran to her aid. He lifted her down from the sink and held her close. "Good girl."

She smiled up at him. "Should we take it all?"

"Yeah. We shouldn't come back here. Is the brick inside?"

Sweetann shrugged, ripped a hole in the bag and looked. She pulled it out. It was intact.

"We should just flush this shit," he said.

"Time?" she said, and shouldered him out of the way. Then she went back and dusted the pink insulation into the toilet, flushed it one more time and then wiped her footprints off with one of Natalie's guest hand towels.

"Let's boogie, babe," Lorenzo said.

At the door, Sweetann stopped and looked at the dead kid, whose ski mask was surely pasted to his face by all that blood. Natalie was nuts if she thought that stain would ever come out of that carpet.

She thought about Nicky, and the image of him being with these guys weakened her knees. "Call the police, Lorenzo. His mother should know."

Lorenzo stepped over the kid while Sweetann waited by the front door, money in the black plastic garbage sack, heroin in the McDonald's bag. In a moment, he came back, and they ran out the front door and down to the car. Just as they got the trunk closed, a black sedan came up behind them.

The same guys that had been at Jack's got out of the car.

"Lorenzo. How odd to find you here."

"Hey, Boingo. What brings you to the finer areas of town? You're quite the traveling man this morning."

"Hardly morning any more, buddy."

Sweetann tightened her grip on the hamburger sack. Boingo walked slowly around the car. Sweetann could feel Lorenzo wind tighter with every second that ticked away. She looked inside and her heart lurched as she saw the butt of the pistol sticking out from between the seats.

"BMW," Boingo said. "Now where's that white Ford?"

"What are you doing here, Boingo?"

"Got a call, happened to be in the neighborhood." He looked up at the house. "This house. Anonymous call. You happen to be the anonymous caller, Lorenzo?"

Lorenzo shook his head. "Nope. Don't know nothing about it."

"Well, why don't you just wait here a few minutes while we see what's going on inside there?"

"Sorry, Boingo, we've got to be going."

"Burgers getting cold?"

Sweetann lifted up the sack and nodded.

"Well, I'm kind of hungry myself." Boingo said, and leaned against the Beamer. "How many burgers you got in there?"

"Lorenzo," Sweetann said. "I've got to go."

"Appointment?" Boingo said. Sweetann ignored him.

Lorenzo threw her the keys. "Take off. I'll catch up with you," he nodded at his Harley.

Sweetann got into the BMW and looked at Boingo. "Do you mind?"

Boingo didn't like any of it, but at least he had Lorenzo. He nodded at the other cop, or pretend cop, and they both backed away from the car.

Sweetann took off. She looked back from a block away and saw Boingo and Lorenzo walking up toward the house.

"Fuck," she said. She hoped to God she'd remember how to find the zoo.

# Chapter 19

Richard balanced a tray of deli sandwiches and cardboard coffees on his knee while he fumbled open the motel room door with its key on the orange tag. The first thing he noticed was that the little envelope of heroin was gone from the nightstand. The second thing he saw was that their luggage had been ransacked, and then he saw Natalie.

She looked dead.

He dropped the tray on the desk and went over to her, fear flaming up inside of him.

"Natalie?"

Her face was pale and translucent. Dark purple circles hung under her eyes all the way to her cheekbones. Her hair was wet from a cloth that had slid from her forehead. Her fingers were limp and cool when he picked them up.

"Natalie?" He felt tears bunch up behind his eyes. He pulled her up by the shoulders, and her head lolled to one side, her mouth hanging open. "Natalie?" The tears began to leak out. He was supposed to leave her. She was supposed to cry and wail and beg him to come back. That was his fantasy.

She was not supposed to die.

He set her down again, put his ear against her breast. Her heart was beating. He gave her little tiny slaps to the cheeks, but that didn't bring her around, it didn't even bring pink up to the surface of her skin. He hauled her back up to a sitting position, shook her a little bit harder. "Natalie!" He held her head up straight by her hair and shouted into her face. "Natalie!"

No response.

He let her flop back down onto the bed, wiped the tears from his face and began to pace. He'd have to take her to the hospital. But then they'd ask questions. They'd arrest her. They might arrest him. It would fuck up all his plans. She would fuck up *all* his plans, the silly bitch. Might get Sweetann and Lorenzo busted, too.

Or, he could just walk away and leave her....

He smacked himself on the forehead with his hand.

He had no options. What kind of a jerk was he to even imagine that he had ever had options? Even though he'd been scheming to get away from her, she was still the woman he had spent ten years with. Some affection had taken hold, in spite of her.

He picked up the telephone and dialed the front desk.

"Front desk."

"Richard Preston, room 208. I need an ambulance."

"Ambulance! They said she was just sick."

Richard took a moment to digest this information. "Who said?"

"Those people. You need an ambulance?"

"What people?"

"The Pickle people."

Richard had to smile, regardless. "They were here? A tall dark haired guy?"

"And a woman. Sweet Pickle."

"They were here and they said she'd be all right?"

"Hey, if you need an ambulance, I'll call one. I don't want nobody dying on my shift."

"They were here and they said she'd be all right?"

"That's what they said."

Richard looked at Natalie's ravaged face. Lorenzo knew about this kind of shit. If he thought she'd be all right...but what if she wasn't?

"I'm going to sit with her for a half hour then, and see if she's better. If she gets worse, then I'll call an ambulance."

"What's the matter with her?"

"I'll call you if I need you."

Richard hung up the phone, took off his shoes and lay on the bed next to Natalie. He pulled her limp body toward him and held her, stroking her stiff, moussed hair. Tension drained out with a few tears, but as soon as the tears stopped, the tension began to build again while he lay there, considering his actions, considering the consequences, considering his bleak, condemned future.

# Chapter 20

"Too much of a coincidence, Lorenzo," Boingo said. "Come with us while we investigate this report."

"I don't know anything," Lorenzo said, his mind whirling. He needed to be with Sweetann. She wouldn't have any idea how to deal with those idiots at the zoo. Those dangerous goddamned idiots.

"You got a key to this place?"

"Nope. You got a warrant?"

Boingo stopped and looked at Lorenzo, who towered over him. "Work with me here, Lorenzo."

"I don't know who you're working for."

"What would make you the most comfortable? Want me to tell you I'm a cop?" Boingo pulled out a badge with an ID card. "I'm a cop. Want me to tell you I work for the airport? I got airport ID here somewhere. Want me to tell you I work for The Cook? I work for The Cook. Which role will make you cooperate with me?"

"I want to get Sweetann's kid back. You get me Sweetann's kid and I'll kiss your feet."

"I got a woman kisses my feet for me. What I want is the money and the dope." He nodded at his partner to stay put, then started walking around to the back door. Lorenzo followed him.

"You get me Sweetann's kid and we'll talk."

"Well, looky here," he said, pointing at the broken pane in the back door. "Let's go inside and see what we find. Maybe there will be a little clue."

Boingo used a handkerchief and reached through the broken glass. Lorenzo hung back, wanting to leave, wanting desperately to leave, but this might be a more direct route to Nicky than through Charles. Trouble was, Sweetann might be handing the dope over to Charles while he hung around Boingo, looking at dead weasels.

"Criminy," Boingo said as he saw the kid leaning up against the wall. Very gently, he lifted the mask until he could make out who it was. "Mikey, Mikey, Mikey," he sighed. "What am I gonna tell your mama?"

Lorenzo stared at all that death and blood in spite of himself. He couldn't take his eyes off it, but Boingo sounded like a bad actor in a bad straight-to-video movie. Boingo put the mask down again over the kid's dead face and elbowed Lorenzo out of the way.

The ringing of the telephone startled both of them and they looked up at it hanging on the kitchen wall. Lorenzo had an eerie feeling it was Mikey calling to tell Boingo what to tell his mama.

"Answer it," Boingo said.

Lorenzo picked up the receiver. "Hello?"

"Lorenzo?"

Lorenzo cupped his hand around the mouthpiece and turned into the corner. "Richard."

"Natalie's real sick, Lorenzo. I'm taking her to the hospital."

This was bad. If Natalie hadn't come around by now, it was probably a good thing she go to the hospital. But still, it might be too late. "Which one?"

"I don't know. The nearest one, I guess," Richard said.

"What's she like? What's she doing?"

"Nothing. It's like she's in a coma."

"Crap."

"I'll take her to Holy Cross."

"We'll meet you there," Lorenzo said.

"Is she going to die?"

"No, Richard, I don't think so."

"Okay, I'm going to go now. I'm going to tell them the truth, you know, about the stuff."

"Just tell them what they need to know. Don't volunteer anything more."

"Will they arrest us?"

"I don't know, Richard, maybe. I don't know. We'll meet you there."

"Okay."

Lorenzo hung up and had no more patience for Boingo and his stupid games.

"If you don't need me, I'm going to take off." He walked

out.

"But I do need you," Boingo said, trying to catch up. "I need us to discuss this little situation you got yourself into and how we can help each other out."

"Real cops are on the way, Boingo."

That did it. Boingo beat Lorenzo out the door.

If Boingo didn't want to wait around to meet the uniforms, then he wasn't as real a cop as he pretended to be. Lorenzo no longer gave a shit about Boingo and that gave him the upper hand again. He walked faster down the driveway and Boingo, with his short legs, had to do double time to keep up. Lorenzo stopped at his motorcycle and pulled the key from his pocket.

"Nothing to discuss," he said, lifting one long leg over the bike and settling down comfortably into the saddle. "First one to get Nicky safe gets the goods."

Boingo and Lorenzo regarded each other, then Lorenzo calmly took sunglasses from his pocket and put them on. He put the key in the Harley and turned it.

"Where you going to be?"

Lorenzo shrugged, gave the starter a kick and the bike roared.

"Here's my card," Boingo said, shoving a card toward Lorenzo's chest.

Lorenzo shouldered him out of the way, slammed the bike into gear and took off down the street. The card fluttered to the ground. Boingo looked at it, then bent over and picked it up, shook off the road dust and put it back in his pocket.

Lorenzo throttled down hard, tension tightening his muscles. It felt good to ride, ride hard, ride fast. He had to get to Sweetann, and he had to get there before she did any serious damage to herself. Natalie had already taken that role.

He didn't want any more casualties in this little escapade, and he had to hurry if he was going to prevent the next one.

# Chapter 21

Sweetann was late, but the black guy's sedan was still there, so she figured she was close enough. She thought about sitting in the car and waiting for Lorenzo. She'd see the black guy if he came out the door and got into his car.

But that wasn't right. She could do this on her own. She could save her son.

She picked up the McDonald's sack, saw that gun butt again, picked it up and put it in the pocket of her hooded sweatshirt. She popped the trunk, lifted out the suitcase and stood quietly, sniffing the air.

She listened, desperately listened for the sound of Lorenzo's motorcycle. She didn't know what to do inside this vast, echoing building. She didn't know if she should just hand over the suitcase, or if she should wait to see Nicky first. She didn't know how to react to these guys, and she was scared. They could overpower her, shoot her, take the dope and that would be that.

The end of Nicky.

God, why were they even messing around with this guy? Why didn't they just give the suitcase to the guy who had Nicky and be done with it?

But who had him? And where?

The whole thing kept Sweetann's head muddled and just shy of aching. She seemed to be so much more centered and in control when Lorenzo was around. This was his universe, not hers. Or at least it had been; she was pretty happy he didn't travel in these circles any more.

Slowly, her feet slogging through the mire of her emotions, she hauled the suitcase and the McDonald's sack to the door of the warehouse, turned the knob and opened it.

The guy turned around at the sound. "It's here," he said into his flat telephone and then folded it up. "Charles has your boy," he said.

"Yeah?" Sweetann said, stopping just inside the door and setting the suitcase on the dusty concrete floor. She shuddered to think of Nicky sitting with that sick, nicotine-stained old man in that bar. "Prove it."

## Chapter 22

Eventually, William brought Nicky two pieces of pizza on a plate. Nicky was starving and wolfed it down. He could have eaten two more. And a cola to go with. But he didn't ask.

Nicky had no illusions about somebody being in trouble somewhere, from the moment that guy William called, with the wind whistling through his teeth. His mom wouldn't work with someone who had a voice and an accent as lowdown as that. That guy was straight out of hoodlum central casting, and when he showed up at their apartment and muscled him and Charlotte into the van, Nicky's suspicions were validated.

Nicky watched a lot of television. Nicky knew all about bad guys. He knew he had to watch his Ps and Qs and not get anybody killed by acting stupid.

But if there was anything that Nicky had learned by being an only child to a guilt-ridden single mother, was this: Kids, if they're smart, can get away with anything.

So Nicky acted like he was about six, mentally. If William thought he was mentally deficient, then Nicky had a big edge. Nick hoped Charlotte would play along.

Nicky liked having an edge.

Charlotte had no edge. Charlotte was round and stupid and started to cry and wail and act like a nerdly woman, something that Nicky knew his mother wasn't doing. So they put her in another room and handed Nicky a fuzzy television with an old Nintendo set and left him to his own devices.

He inspected his prison cell. It was not much. Standard, tract-home bedroom, not nearly as nice as his cool upstairs bedroom at home. There was a twin sized bed, the TV, a dresser, a closet, and windows that, he discovered upon closer inspection, had been nailed shut. A telephone jack, but no phone. They brought a cell phone to him when they wanted him to call his mom.

It would be easy to escape; just break a window and take off. But that wouldn't be smart, Nicky decided, because he didn't know where he was or where to go, besides the police.

And something told him that his mom wouldn't want him to do that, not just yet. These guys might hurt his mom if he did something like that.

He was less than an hour from home, so they were still in the Seattle area. He was okay.

Besides, escaping through a broken window would be the expected thing. He wanted to do the unexpected thing. He assumed he'd know what that was when the time came.

So he sat tight. He ate the Pizza Hut pizza that was delivered (he noted the time; surely Pizza Hut kept records), he played the video games, he memorized every identifiable feature he could see out the bedroom window, and in William's ugly face.

And he played to William's level, which was about six years old, too. He whined about not being allowed to play with the dog, and he used kindergarten vocabulary when he wanted to go to the toilet. He shouted for Charlotte whenever they let him out, and she shouted back, so he knew she was still alive and feisty.

The more he thought about it, the more he realized how easy it would be for him to wiggle out of this situation—but he had his mom to consider, and Charlotte too, he guessed, so until he knew more, he'd just sit tight and try not to worry about her.

He wished she had a boyfriend, or a husband. He wished she had a man to take care of her.

# Chapter 23

Richard hung up the phone and then sat and looked at Natalie. Her bloodless, borderline-anorexic, alcoholic face looked dead already, and he wondered if he might not be doing her a favor to just let her quietly give up her tortured life. Natalie wasn't having a lot of fun. She always wanted more than she could have, which was a good thing, but she whatever she set her eyes on, she didn't go about getting it with steady unwavering persistence, she wanted it with a clawing, clutching vengeance. She always felt *entitled* to whatever she wanted. And if her desires were denied, she raged.

She was one unhappy woman, and she made his life pretty awful in the process.

He was tired of it all, too. He'd made his escape plan, had even begun to execute it. Being so deceptive made him feel lowdown and underhanded, but after living with Natalie so long, he knew there was only one course of action to take if he was going to get out of this marriage intact, and with a dime he could call his own. It wasn't nice, but his situation was desperate.

And then she'd started up with the baby thing again. That was the last thing they needed.

No, Richard needed to make a clean getaway, and what could be cleaner than a wife who died of her excesses? He could just sit here at her bedside and wait for her to breathe her last, then heroically throw her into the car and take her to the hospital, a grieving husband's valiant effort at saving his addicted wife's life.

But he had to time it right; he couldn't take her in if she were already cold.

Besides, he'd already talked to the motel clerk.

*You bastard,* he said to himself.

He stood up, bounced up and down on the balls of his feet a few times, trying to figure out what course of action to take. Then he knew. Of course he knew. He hurried into the bathroom, filled the tub with cold water, then dumped in all the towels.

*I'm not a very nice guy, but I'll be damned if I'll let you turn me into a sleazebag who lets his wife die of an overdose right in front of him.*

While the towels were soaking, he went back into the bedroom and took off all Natalie's clothes, a task more difficult than usual. Generally speaking, when he had to undress her, she was just drunk, and could move this way and that and help him out. Now, she was freakishly heavy, something that made his heart pound with worry.

Then he slogged a cold, dripping bath towel across the motel room floor and threw it on top of her.

She gasped.

He put another one on her legs and feet, then took the warmed one off her torso and replaced it with two heavy, fresh, ice-cold ones. Her eyes, unfocused and bloodshot, popped open. She began to make noises.

Relentless, Richard threw one over her face and she began to fight.

It was working.

He felt an angry relief.

He scraped the wet mess off her onto the floor, held her, even as she fought him. She wanted to go back to sleep, and as long as he knew she was capable of consciousness, he was willing to let her. He covered her up with the damp motel bedspread and dialed their house.

No answer. He left a message on the machine for Lorenzo, but he was probably already on the way to the hospital. Oh well. He'd figure it out.

Lorenzo and Sweetann had probably taken off with all of the cash. Good for them.

Richard sat on the bed next to Natalie, and fingered her stiff and sticky hair. He'd put up with a lot of crap from this woman, that was for sure, and thoughts of homicide and divorce were never too far from his mind. He was going to leave her, and soon.

But as scummy as he was, he knew now that he was no murderer.

Richard closed his eyes next to his smacked-up wife and

wondered what in the hell was going to happen next. He hated being the one who had to just sit and wait. He felt as though all the other players were acting out his life while he sat and waited for them to tell him how it was turning out.

One of these days, Richard would be a player.

He rubbed a forefinger over Natalie's forehead and watched her eyes move under thin, dusky lids.

One of these days. Soon.

He unwrapped a tuna salad sandwich and popped the lid off one of the coffees, then sat back and watched Natalie twitch while he ate.

# Chapter 24

"Where's your boyfriend?" the black guy asked.

"He's coming," Sweetann said. "Where is my son?"

"He's coming too," the guy said with a nasty smile. "He'll be here." He started walking closer. "Let's take a look at what you brought me."

"Not a chance," Sweetann said, and stood her ground. She put her hands in her pockets and hoped that the fool could see the muzzle of the revolver outlined through the fabric without her having to face him down with it.

He saw it.

"How come Lorenzo isn't with you?"

"He had other business."

"I don't like it."

"I don't care what you like or don't like. I want my boy."

"Just a minute." The guy turned away from her, opened his phone and dialed. He walked clear to the other side of the empty warehouse, speaking softly, the sounds reverberating back to Sweetann like some kind of singing whale echoes.

Sweetann's heart pumped. So many things could go wrong. One bad move, one mispronounced word and Nicky would vanish. She stood there, watching the black guy and she felt bone tired. Weary. Weary of motherhood and shouldering its massive responsibilities alone, weary of loneliness and being broke and the search for not only a suitable mate, but a suitable father for her son....

Weary. Weary of doing it all herself.

And now she'd brought *this* whole stupid thing down on their heads.

*Well, God, if you just get us through this one—*

She resisted the impulse to bark a laugh. It came out like a hiccup and she saw two beads of saliva sail through the dusty space. Yeah, here she was, making deals with God again, like she did every time she tried to pay her bills with the inadequate little paycheck she got twice a month. That was just like her.

But the truth was, if she got through this one intact, maybe she'd be a little more willing to accept her role as single mom. She could use a little excitement in her life, it was true, but this was the wrong type.

There was no such thing as a big score, she realized. And she wasn't the type of person that the universe would gift with a winning lottery ticket. No, her lot in life was to work hard, day by day and do the best that she could, and try to be a good person. For the most part, she'd done that, but now...

She would, by God, be happy to be back in her crummy little apartment with her stellar kid again. She couldn't wait to get back to normal, even if normal sometimes seemed like desperation. With increased risk comes increased reward, Lorenzo had said. She would be happy with safe from here on out. She'd never take normal for granted again.

The man turned around and walked back to her, holding out the phone.

Sweetann's heart began to pound harder, but she made no move toward him. She remembered what Lorenzo said, and made him walk all the way to her.

She took the phone.

"Hello?"

"Mom?" That cry of one's cub. Sweetann wanted to dissolve into it, but she held her cool. Just one more minute.

"Are you in LA?"

"Seattle. Hey. Ow." Disconnect.

*NO!* Sweetann wanted to scream. More! I need to talk to him some more. She held on to the dead telephone with a powerful grip. She wanted to reassure herself that he was okay.

He was okay. She knew it by the tenor of his voice. When Nicky was hurt, or scared, his voice did a little quavering thing. Or he would have whined. He was fine. He was alert, and defiant.

He was fine. He was a wise little sonofabitch, too. Took after his too-smart daddy. He didn't even miss a beat with that question, are you in LA. Quick mind. And he was still in Seattle. Well. That changed things.

Reluctantly, she eased her grip, slowly folded the phone and held it out to the guy. "Sorry," she said. "We were disconnected."

She knew what to do. She had to do what was not expected

of a young mother in trouble. She couldn't let these guys peg her, anticipate her, predict her.

She picked up the suitcase and the McDonald's sack with one hand, leaving the other on the revolver in her pocket.

"Wait," he said, punching numbers into the phone again.

"Nah," she said. "I'll be in touch."

As she walked out into the afternoon sun, she heard him say, "Get that kid here. Now."

She smiled, feeling in charge. They were going to bring Nicky to her. She was calling the shots now.

Wasn't she?

She put the suitcase and the McDonald's bag back into the trunk of the BMW, got in and drove away from the warehouse.

Two blocks later, she began to shake. Then the tears came. She pulled over and let them consume her.

# Chapter 25

"You little shit," William snarled.

Nicky wanted to spit in his face, but he cringed instead, acting the part of the dumb little kid. "I'm sorry," he said. "I'm sorry. What did I do?"

"I oughtta—"

"Please don't take away the video games," Nicky said, acting contrite, finding it hard to keep a straight face.

Just like in the cartoons, William looked over at the little television. "The video games, huh? That's exactly what I'm going to—"

The phone rang in his hand. He looked at Nicky with a "stay put and shut up" look, or at least his clichéd version of it, and pushed the button. "Yeah." He listened. His eyebrows went up. "Now?" He listened. He scowled. "How?" He listened. He stood up straighter. "What about the girl?" He listened. His eyes narrowed. He smiled. "Gotcha," he said, and pushed the button to disconnect.

"Pack your shit," he said. "We're going to the airport."

Nicky perked up. "Really? Are we going somewhere? I've never been in an airplane before."

"We're going to LA."

"LA? Dude! Can we go to Disneyland? Can we take the video games with?"

William didn't know how to respond to that. "Just sit tight for a few minutes, while I call the...make the...get the..." He clenched his fist in frustration, his breath making a whipping sound as it whooshed in and out between his teeth. "Just wait here." He left the bedroom, locking the door behind him.

Nicky sat down on the bed. He wasn't sure what to make of all this, except that his mom was in LA, so going to LA couldn't be a bad thing. It was going to get him closer to her. He wanted to be closer to her.

He wanted to be with her.

He missed her.

He thought for a minute that he was going to cry, but that

wouldn't do. He'd need to keep himself together, keep his act up for this. Chances are, there would be bigger challenges to come than William and all of these stupid video games combined, and if his mom were in danger, he'd need to be very aware.

Maybe, after they got rid of the bad guys, he and his mom could go to Disneyland.

He scooted up the bed until his back was against the wall and waited. He had nothing to pack, so he was already ready.

He sat there and waited. Waiting was hard, but he was wondering about the answer to William's question, "What about the girl?"

He lay down, and eventually slept.

William turned on the light and Nicky jumped up, startled, disoriented.

William grabbed him by the arm, hustled him out of the house and out into a cold, Pacific Northwest drizzle.

The Mexican guy who had driven the van when Charlotte and Nicky were snatched was in the driver's seat again. William opened the side door and muscled Nicky inside, where he sat on the dirty metal floor next to a blanket-covered form. William slammed the door, jumped in the front seat and they took off. Some Snapple bottles rattled around in the back, echoing in the big, empty space.

Nicky knew that Charlotte was under the blanket, but he was afraid to touch her. He was afraid to look.

He wanted to touch her, he wanted to touch Charlotte real bad, to see if she was warm or cold.

The Mexican guy opened his window and ashes from his cigarette flew into the back of the van. Nicky ducked down to get out of the wind, and his hand came down on Charlotte's foot.

There. He'd touched her.

He sneaked a hand under the blanket and found her leg. It was warm.

He snorted with relief, loud enough so that William turned around and looked at him.

"Mind yourself," William said, "Or you'll look like that."

Nicky feigned horror. "Charlotte?" he asked William.

William nodded.

"Is she dead?" he asked, feeling genuinely wide-eyed.

"Not yet," William said, then grinned, showing those big old fence post teeth. Then he turned around again, and he and the Mexican started talking about something, but Nicky couldn't understand them.

He scooted around and put his hand under the blanket again. He found Charlotte's arm. He squeezed it, but it felt funny, like it had no life. He dug his fingernails in, hard, trying to get a response, but there was nothing. Maybe she wasn't dead, but she was pretty close to it.

The van took a radical right hand turn, slamming Nicky against the metal side.

"Sorry," William said, looking back. Then he looked down at Charlotte, and Nicky looked down at Charlotte and he saw that the blanket had come off her face when he was thrown against the side, and she did indeed look dead.

"What's the matter with her?" Nicky asked.

"She's sick," William said, then laughed and turned back toward the front.

"She can't go to LA like this," Nicky said, then looked out the window and noticed they weren't on the freeway at all, but out by some cow pasture or something with wire fences.

"She ain't going with us," William said. "She was—whatcha say—uncooperative. So while we go to LA and have a good time, the girl here, she's going to stay here and do a little...um...grazing." He and the Mexican laughed it up good that time.

"Charlotte," Nicky said, turning her face toward him. It was pale, very pale. Even her lips were white and icky looking. He touched her cheek, but it had that same lifeless feeling that her arm had.

He pulled her toward him and saw bruises and needle marks in the crook of her arm.

Hate for William blossomed in his belly. Rage began to burn inside his chest.

*Calm down*, he told himself. *Calm down.*

He took a couple of deep breaths, knowing that his time was coming. He'd get even with this guy for hurting Charlotte. He'd get good and even.

The Mexican pulled the van off to the side of the road and

stopped.

Nicky stood up and looked out the window. They were on some country lane. No houses, no cars, nothing but some cows on the other side of the fence.

This was not a good place to escape. There was no place to escape to.

Besides, they were taking him to see his mom. He had to be patient and do the right thing. The smart thing.

William got out, came around and opened the sliding door. He got inside, squatted down, grabbed Charlotte by the armpits and dragged her toward the door.

"What are you doing?" Nicky asked, panic beginning to build. He was forgetting all that he had to do in order to remain calm and alive. He liked Charlotte. He loved Charlotte. He'd known her ever since he could remember, and now it looked like these guys were going to kill her. "Please don't hurt her. Please don't."

The Mexican grabbed Charlotte's feet and, suspended between them like a hammock, they began to swing her. Once, twice, three times and they let her go. She flew through the air and then landed with a splash and a whoosh of the lungs in the bottom of the drainage ditch that ran along the road.

"No," Nicky said. "No, please don't leave her there. It's wet. She'll die."

"You're right," William said, then unzipped his pants.

"Hey, no, man," the Mexican said.

"I'm just gonna piss," William said, but it was obvious where he was going to aim.

"Do it over there, man," the Mexican said, nodding his head toward the other side of the road. "DNA, you know?"

"Yeah, I know. Of course I know," William said, and walked to the other side of the road.

Nicky looked up at the Mexican kid. He was a kid, too, not more than twenty. William was old, probably thirty or thirty-five, but this guy... "You're not really going to leave her here to die, are you?"

The Mexican looked at Nicky, then reached out and ruffled his hair. "Orders," he said. "We follow orders. You'll learn about that some day."

Nicky jerked back. He didn't want this guy touching him. "But she's my friend."

"Sorry. She was a pain in the ass."

William came back around, zipping up.

"Pick better friends," the Mexican said.

"C'mon," William said. "Let's fly." He shoved Nicky back into the van and slammed the door.

Nicky knelt, hands on the side window, but from where he was, he couldn't see Charlotte down in the ditch.

He sat down hard when the kid made a u-turn, and hugged the blanket. He buried his face in it and started to cry. He didn't want to cry, he wanted to be an adult. He knew his mom needed him to be a man, she needed him to take care of her, but right now he was a scared little boy and that's all he wanted to be.

He sobbed quietly, because he didn't want William and the Mexican to hear him. He sobbed for Charlotte and he sobbed for his lonely mom and he prayed. He prayed that Charlotte would wake up and crawl out of that wet ditch. He prayed that some farmer would come along and save her.

He prayed that somebody would save him, too. Somebody tall, and handsome, and brave. Somebody with black hair and blue eyes, just like in the comics. Some super hero who would swoop down, see him in trouble and save him. Somebody who would see how beautiful his mom was and the two of them would fall in love at first sight.

Please, God.

Please hurry.

Nicky curled up in the blanket as the van sped off.

# Chapter 26

Charles heard the front door of the bar slam open and he knew who was coming. He didn't have to stand up and look over the back of the leatherette booth to know that The Cook was pissed off.

And sure enough, a moment later, Charles heard the unmistakable voice.

"Stay here," The Cook growled to his goons, and a moment later, appeared at Charles's table.

Charles nodded in acknowledgement, and pointed toward the red leatherette seat across from him. It was an invitation to sit. The Cook looked at it with distaste, as if he'd like to have it sanitized before he put his ass onto it, then he slid onto the bench seat opposite Charles.

Charles calmly put a matchbook cover in his paperback, took off his glasses, rubbed his watery eyes and then looked up at his guest.

"What the fuck happened, Charles?"

"These are nice people, Cookie. They're not hoods, they're not thugs. You can't strong-arm them and you can't lie to them. What they want is simple: the kid. You give them the kid, they'll give you the dope. Why do you want to make it more complicated than that?"

"It *is* more complicated than that. There's William."

Charles calmly tipped the old cigarette butt into the ashtray and lit another one. He took a deep drag, then set the cigarette down. "William is easily replaced."

"And the airport."

"The airport is no threat. They're just beating their chests and scratching their balls. Don't worry about the airport."

"No doubt the cops are after them by now, too," Cook said. "And Lorenzo. Shit. Who knows what they might do? They're scared. They're amateurs. They might just take the money and throw the goods into the ocean."

Charles knew that this booth in this bar was probably the only place The Cook could break down and mutter, panic-stricken, about all his worries. Everywhere else, he had to be the big guy, in charge. Charles didn't mind. He'd been around a lot longer, anyway. He could help The Cook settle down, and maybe he could save Lorenzo in the process.

"They might," he said. "But you still have the boy."

"If we lose that shipment—"

Charles whipped out a hand and gripped The Cook's wrist. "Stop it," he said, a whispered command so forceful that The Cook stopped whimpering and looked him straight in the eye. "The boy is on his way here. Lorenzo trusts me. You keep your goons away from him and his girlfriend, and everything will be all right."

The Cook took a shuddering sigh. Sometimes he looked like a little boy.

"Now," Charles went on. "I want nothing to happen to Lorenzo and the girl. Or the kid. I want us to get the shipment, I want them to keep the money, and I want you to teach your thugs a few manners."

"Keep the money?" The Cook looked like he was going to have a heart attack. "You want them to keep the money?"

"Yes. I want them to keep the money. It's a small price to pay for what you had that girl go through at the zoo. Sometimes I think you've got no sense."

"Keep the money?" The Cook couldn't seem to understand the concept.

Charles was losing patience. "Lorenzo's cleaned himself up. There's a lot to be said for that. And we're selling our souls to the devil every goddamned time somebody sticks a dirty needle in their vein. It isn't often we can help a guy out. Yes, they keep the money, they get the kid, we leave them alone."

The Cook sat back and took a deep sigh.

Charles narrowed his eyes. "Okay?"

The Cook nodded slowly. "Yeah, okay."

"Okay," Charles said, and reached for his paperback book, dismissing The Cook. "Lorenzo trusts me. He'll be in touch. You get that kid and take him to the zoo, and you wait."

The Cook kept nodding, slowly, absent-mindedly. He looked as if he had been beaten, and he wasn't used to that.

"Okay?"

"Yeah," The Cook said. "Okay." He pulled back into himself, took a deep breath, sat up straight, then slid halfway out of the booth.

"Lorenzo trusts me, Cookie," Charles said to his book, "And I'm trusting you to do the right thing here. The boy arrives LAX at six-forty. You better get there early."

The Cook nodded, and left, picking up his hoods on the way out.

Charles opened his paperback and pretended to read, but in the back of his mind was The Cook's mean streak and his relentless insubordination. Charles hoped The Cook was going to just do as he was told. Charles hoped he wasn't going to have to teach The Cook a severe lesson.

Because he could.

And he would.

But he didn't want to. He wanted The Cook to behave, and he wanted this situation to dissolve.

# Chapter 27

The Cook got into the car and looked at his watch. He had hours to kill before the kid arrived at LAX. And he had a little passion to spend, too.

He clenched and unclenched his fists. Fucking Charles acted like he owned the joint, like he still controlled the operation. Charles was a withered up old carcass, and he needed to remember his place in the scheme of things. His place was not to be bossing everybody around.

Fucking Charles.

"Take me home," The Cook said to the driver, and the sedan sped off toward the suburbs.

The Cook opened the gate with a remote control he kept in his pocket, and when the car was parked in the drive, he told his boys to wait. Then he jumped out and walked around to the front entrance.

Before he entered the house, he turned around and looked at them. The two guys, with their sunglasses on, were lighting cigarettes. In a moment, they'd be leaning against the car. Out of some perverted sense of respect, he knew they were holding off their discussion of his sex life until he was out of earshot.

Jesus. They even looked like thugs.

The Cook was sick of his life. He hated his life. He hadn't known it until just now, when he got a snapshot of his frustration about to be taken out on the simple woman who did nothing but obey him, and the two idiots leaning up against a shiny black sedan in his driveway. He looked like the fucking Mafia; why did he feel like such an angry goddamned little kid?

He strode through the house, seeing a pack of cigarettes sitting in a clean ashtray on the coffee table. Felicia better not be smoking again. He hated the smell of cigarettes on her breath.

She was reading out by the pool. She was wearing a big floppy hat, sunglasses, and a bikini bottom, her dark skin oily and shiny.

She looked up as he opened the sliding glass door. "Uh-oh," she said. "Daddy's had a hard day."

He wanted to cry, he wanted to melt into her arms and sob. Instead, he pulled off his tie, unbuttoned his shirt, kicked off his shoes, and left a trail of clothing from the house to her chaise lounge. "Help me out here, babe," he said, collapsing naked in the sun on the chair next to her.

She slowly got up, took off her sunglasses and her hat, picked up the sun-warmed tanning oil and squirted some into her hand. Then she rubbed it over her brown breasts, moving in a silent dance, pinching up her nipples until they were erect. She oiled up her belly, her eyes searching his face, watching him watch her.

He liked it; he loved it, it distracted him for a moment, but it didn't help.

It helped her, though. She knew the gardener was in the cabaña. He was probably watching. She liked that a lot, and did some slow bumps and grinds, looking at The Cook, but feeling the heat of the gardener's eyes on her butt.

She moved both oily hands slowly down her tummy and slid them into her bikini bottom, and moved her head back in true pleasure as she did to herself something The Cook never did to her any more. Something she would like the gardener to begin doing on a regular basis.

It felt good, it felt real good, and she opened her eyes and saw that her husband enjoyed watching, too, but it didn't help.

"Please, Felicia," he said, and keeping her face from showing the disgust she had come to associate with their one-sided sex, she brought her juicy fingers out of her pants, put one of them in his mouth, wiped another one across his nose, then she knelt on the concrete and took his flaccid little penis into her mouth and tried to do something with it.

"C'mon, daddy," she said, trying to make it sound breathless and hot. She worked it with lips, teeth and fingers. "C'mon, daddy, fuck me. I want you to fuck me hard. Hard and fast."

"I will, too, you little bitch," The Cook said, sweat running off his forehead. "I'm going to fuck you so hard—"

Then it happened. Just like always. His little pecker zoomed to its pitifully erect size, "Oh," he said, "*Oh!*" and a little glob of semen leaked out of its end. Then it shrank back to normal.

Subnormal.

Felicia had never seen anything like it.

"Oh god, babe, that was perfect," he said.

She sat down on the concrete, rested her elbow on his knees, and she watched him with the usual disillusionment and amazement. He lay there, eyes closed. She wiped her hand on the edge of her towel and wondered what the gardener thought about that.

Then The Cook got up and dove into the pool. She put on her hat and her sunglasses and went back to her chaise and her book.

He took long strokes through the cool water, then climbed out. Refreshed, he grabbed a soft towel from the stack by the door, wrapped it around his waist and went inside to take a nap.

# Chapter 28

"Mikey's dead and the shipment is still missing?" The voice on the other end of the line was not happy. From where Boingo stood, he could see the end of his career. Perhaps he'd go the way of Mikey, except out in some desert, not in some nice house.

Boingo pulled at his shirt collar. He opened his mouth to speak into the phone, but Mr. Hunter beat him to it.

"This is not the way you pay off your debts, Boingo."

"Yeah, I know, listen, it was kind of a misunderstanding. I know this guy, though, we go way back."

"You and me, we go way back too, don't we Boingo?"

"Yeah, but this guy—"

"Your loyalties, Boingo, where are your loyalties?"

"I want to pay you, Mr. Hunter, no shit, I do. And I will. This guy, he's going to give me the stuff, but he has this girlfriend, and her kid—"

"I'll tell you what."

Boingo shielded the telephone from traffic sounds. He didn't want to miss a word. He couldn't afford to get anything else wrong.

"You're a pretty worthless human being, and I would lose not one second of sleep if you happened to fall off a bridge, but I'd like my money back from you first. I'm not going to get that if you're food for the crabs."

Mr. Hunter took a long pause.

Boingo loosened his tie.

"So here's a tip, Boingo. Your buddy's girlfriend's kid arrives at the airport at six-forty. You get the kid, and then you get the shipment, you hear me?"

Boingo nodded, squeaked out a reply, cleared his voice, then said, "Yeah."

"Now I'm being very generous with you, time-wise here, Boingo. Just like I been very generous with you money-wise. You're over your deadline and you're over your creditline and I still have to call Mikey's mother. But I'm giving you a break.

Until nine tonight. Come nine o'clock tonight, Boingo, I don't have my money or my shipment, somebody'll be talking to *your* mother, you understand me?"

"Yeah."

"We understand each other then."

"Yeah."

"Six-forty from Seattle."

"Yeah, okay, fine," Boingo said, but he said it to a dead phone because Mr. Hunter clicked off as soon as he was finished speaking.

Boingo rubbed his forehead. He wanted to find Lorenzo and his girlfriend and take them with him to the airport. The girl could get the kid, Boingo could get the suitcase, and all would be hunky-fucking-dory.

So where was he going to find Lorenzo?

His phone chirped. He opened it and punched the button. "Yeah?"

"Boingo?"

At last he had an underling to berate. "How nice of you to fucking check in with me. Where the hell have you been?"

"I..."

"Spare me. Where's Lorenzo?"

"He was at the house—"

"He was, but he ain't no more."

"Then try Holy Cross Hospital. He thinks I'm taking Natalie there. I might have to."

"What about the blonde?"

"I don't know about her."

"How the fuck did you lose control of the shipment, Richard? You want to tell me that? How the fuck did you do that?" Boingo took a deep breath.

"I knew nothing about a shipment, Boingo. You told me to pick up that suitcase, but you never told me anything else. It came at a bad time, because my sister had just arrived. I grabbed it instead of my sister's suitcase, figuring we'd just go back for hers, but once my wife saw what was inside—"

"Never mind," Boingo said. "The kid comes in at LAX at six-forty. You get him and take him to the zoo. AND, I want Lorenzo and the blonde girl both there to make the trade. You got that?"

"No way. We're square."

"Square?" Boingo slammed his fist against the side of the Seven-Eleven. "How the fuck do you figure that?"

"I had to do one thing for you, just one, and I did it. That was our deal."

"Yeah, well you fucked it up."

"Not my fault, Boingo. We're finished, you and me. Our business is concluded."

"You listen to me, you little cocksucker," Boingo said. "The whole world is in a cluster fuck at the moment. You're not off the hook with me until I'm off the hook with that goddamned shipment. You help me square this with Mr. Hunter and then, and only then, will I keep your goddamned secret. Otherwise I'm going to have a little talk with The Cook."

There was silence on the other line.

"Yeah, all right. I'll... I'll see what I can do. My wife..."

"*Fuck her*!" Yelling at somebody else made Boingo feel a little bit better. "I don't care about your goddamned wife, Richard. Six-forty. I suggest you get there early, and we can conclude this goddamned transaction before it disturbs my digestion even more."

"Yeah... okay."

Boingo clicked off the phone. Shit runs downhill, he thought, and at last he was standing one step above the guy at the bottom.

"Holy Cross Hospital," he told the guy driving. "And keep an eye out for Lorenzo on that Harley."

# Chapter 29

Sweetann was just fixing her face in the visor mirror when she heard the rumble of the Harley, and looked up just in time to see Lorenzo flash right by her on his way to the zoo. It made her want to start crying all over again.

She was too tired, too worried about Nick, too over-the-edge about Lorenzo, too everything. She needed a nice long sleep. But that wouldn't come until she had Nicky back. At least now she was certain that he was all right. She was probably going to see him, hold him, hug him, kiss him, have him back safely with her within a few hours, but until that actually happened, she was strung so tight she could feel every nerve vibrate and sizzle with tension and regret.

She just needed to remember that what these guys wanted was the dope and the money. They didn't want Nicky. As long as she had control of the stuff, Nicky would be all right.

That was a hard thought to keep in the front of her mind.

And now she had to go chase down Lorenzo, before he burst into that damned warehouse and damaged...damaged what? Damaged whatever there was to damage. She couldn't even think any more. Strategies were never her long suit. Not in chess, or poker, or marriage. With Sweetann, what you see is what you get.

Deception was a trait she found fascinating in others, but could never pull off convincingly in herself. She couldn't do it. She didn't want to do it. She never again wanted to be put in a position to deal with those who thrived on caginess, deception and trickery. Especially when the stakes were so high.

She took a deep breath, looked at her red and swollen eyes one more time, then she put her sunglasses on just in case she actually caught up with Lorenzo, and started the car.

But he pulled up behind her before she pulled out into the road.

He leaned the bike on its kickstand, took off his helmet and ran his hands through his hair. He looked long and lean and cool and sweet in those leathers.. He swung one of those amazing legs over the seat, set the helmet on it and walked over to her, taking off his shades as he walked. She just wanted to Velcro herself to his side.

And she would. They didn't need to separate again, not until this damned thing was finished. She and Lorenzo would become a unit.

Starting now.

She fumbled with the door handle, but it was different in a BMW, and she broke a nail, then those damned tears were back again.

He opened the door and she fumbled with her seat belt, and then he lifted her up and out and held her and she sobbed and sobbed, all the worry over Nicky and the stress of her life draining out onto his jacket.

He just held her, not talking, not shushing her, not stroking her, nothing. His long arms just enfolded her and held her close.

Soon she felt the calm heat of him right through their clothes and the tears spent themselves, and then there was just Sweetann, emotionally and intellectually naked.

Lorenzo seemed to like her that way, too.

His acceptance of her weakness left a certain satisfaction at the end of the emotional storm. The tears weren't spent in frustration and her soul left wanting. The tears were released and her soul was recharged with Lorenzo's reassurance. When she was ready to wipe her face and blow her nose, he kissed the hair at her temple and let her go.

They got back into the car. He picked up her hand and held it with both of his while she told him what had happened, and that Nicky was on his way to LA.

He told her that Richard was taking Natalie to the hospital.

Funny, how little she cared about Natalie.

She took a deep breath, rubbed at her raw eyes and finally looked up at him, squinting in shame at the way she looked.

"Want to go to the hospital?" Lorenzo asked.

"No. Richard can take care of her." She untangled her hand from his, and blew her nose, then began twisting the damp tissue into a fraying rope. "I don't want to answer any more questions, Lorenzo. I'm so tired. I'm so worried about Nicky and I'm just so goddamned tired."

"Follow me," he said.

"Where?"

"Back to Jack's. Nicky won't be here for hours yet. We can get some sleep, then we'll go to the airport and meet every plane in from Seattle."

Sweetann smiled shyly. It sure felt good to have someone else calling the shots for a change.

She looked up at him, her swollen eyes feeling scratchy and froggy.

It felt good to be taken care of.

She wanted him to take care of her for the rest of her life.

# Chapter 30

Nicky kept his eyes open and his mouth shut at Sea-Tac airport. The William geek didn't even have to tell him. He noticed where all the security guards were, he noticed where all the emergency exits were, he scanned each person he passed, looking for a familiar face.

At first, he was embarrassed to be seen with this guy, afraid that somebody might think that he was William's son or something, but then he realized there were more important things to be concerned with. He'd play along. He had his mom to think about. He didn't want to do anything to get her hurt.

He'd never forget what they did to Charlotte.

He stayed alert, waiting for an opportunity to do the unexpected.

After sitting for what seemed like hours in the gate area, watching weird people and picking at the hole in his tennis shoe, they finally boarded. The pretty flight attendant stuck some plastic wings to his shirt and gave him a toothy smile, and he knew he could go to her for help. She was an adult; she had authority.

A plan began to form in his mind.

William wanted to sit by the window, so Nicky let him. He sat in the middle seat, but when they closed the doors, and nobody was on the aisle, Nicky moved over.

William gave him a look.

"What?" Nick asked. "Where am I going to go?" They buckled in and settled back. The plane took off, Nicky fantasizing that he was in a space capsule, enduring 8Gs, headed for Mars.

William had bought their tickets with cash, and when the flight attendants pushed their ugly metal cart down the aisle, William flashed some bills and got a double vodka and a beer.

"Is the beer for me?" Nicky asked, but William just scowled at him. Nicky got a ginger ale.

He watched carefully as William poured the two little bottles of vodka over the ice, then drank them.

"William?" Nicky asked.

"What?"

"Has my mom done something wrong?"

"She stole something from my boss," he said without making eye contact.

"No way. Stole something? My mom? What did she steal?"

"Product."

"What kind of product?"

"Drink your soda."

"Is she in trouble?"

"Yep," William said. "Bad trouble."

Nicky's stomach rumbled with this information, and he had to consciously take a breath. "Are you guys going to...you know...what you did to Charlotte? Are you going to do that to my mom?"

William turned and looked at him, his fishy eyes serious. "There's always that possibility. I don't like thieves, do you?"

"It's a mistake," Nicky said. "My mom doesn't steal. She would never."

Nicky put his head down and kicked at the seat in front of him until the lady in that seat turned around and asked him nicely to stop.

"What about me? If you hurt her, what will happen to me?" This line of questioning started out as an information gathering session, but suddenly Nicky wasn't sure of anything. They might just leave him by the side of the road, too— homeless, an orphan—with nowhere to go.

"I don't know, boy. You're only my responsibility until this plane touches down in LA." He finished sucking the last of the vodka from the ice cubes, then popped open the beer. "Let's hope she sees you, sees the error of her ways, and gives us back what she took."

"Drugs," Nicky said. "You guys are drug dealers, aren't you?"

"Drink your soda." He reached into the seat pocket and pulled out the in-flight catalog. "Here. Read something."

Nicky elbowed the magazine aside. "Drugs," he said. "I hope she throws it all into the sewer." He found headphones in the seat pocket, put them on, plugged into the armrest and punched buttons until he found some country music.

He needed to think.

They weren't going to take him to his mom. They were going to dangle him as a carrot for her to come to them. If she had something of theirs, she took it for good reason, and for Nicky to be cooperating with them was the exact wrong thing for him to do.

So he had to do the unexpected.

Lunch came, but Nicky had no appetite. William wolfed down a sandwich in a box and asked for another beer.

As soon as the cart was out of the center aisle, Nicky took off his headphones and unbuckled his seat belt. It was time to set his plan in motion.

"Where you going?" William asked, his big hand hard on Nicky's shoulder.

"To the bathroom."

William tried to sit up and look over the back of the seats, but his seat belt held him down and he almost dumped his lunch tray in the process. He looked down at it. "Make it fast," he said.

Nicky got out of the seat and wandered slowly to the back of the plane.

The attendant with the nice smile was poking errant strands of hair underneath a hair pin. She looked like the girl who played Maria in The Sound of Music last year at the high school, when he played one of the von Trapp kids.

He ducked into the kitchen and out of William's line of sight.

"Can I talk to you for a minute?" Nicky asked.

"Sure, hon," she said, gave the pin an extra-tight shove, then squatted down to his eye level. She smiled warmly at him and if Nicky hadn't been so nervous about the ramifications of what he was about to set into motion, he could have fallen in love with her. "What can I do for you?" she asked.

# Chapter 31

"Do you think Boingo will come back here?" Sweetann asked.

"No. And it's okay if he does."

Lorenzo parked his bike around the side of the guest cottage, then got into the car with Sweetann. The gate closed securely behind them. Sweetann felt too weak to move.

"You know," Sweetann said, nodding to herself. "I have a good feeling about Nicky. He's a bright kid." She smoothed the nap down on Lorenzo's leather-covered knee. "I wish you knew him."

"Me, too."

The car ticked as it cooled and the two of them sat quietly, enjoying the intimacy of the quiet space, although without the air conditioning, the car was beginning to heat up.

"You will. He's a smart kid. If anybody can do the right thing by being smart, Nicky will. It's scary sometimes, how smart that kid is." She looked up at Lorenzo, but then looked right down again, not wanting him to see her swollen eyes. "I have way more confidence in him than I do in Richard and Natalie."

Lorenzo snorted out his agreement. It didn't take much to surpass Richard and Natalie in common sense. A ten-year-old was likely smarter than those two.

They were quiet together for a long time. Then one of Lorenzo's long fingers began to pet the back of her hand, which rested quietly on his knee. She turned it over, and he stroked her palm.

"Some weekend, eh?"

Sweetann took a ragged breath, and nodded.

"Ready for a nap?"

"Cuddle."

"Yeah. Me, too. Should we take the stuff inside?"

She shook her head. "Let somebody steal it," she said. "I'm sick of it."

He smiled, reached over and kissed her cheek.

They got out of the car, went into the cottage, which was cool and silent. Sweetann was so tired, and yet so jangled—she felt like she had in college, when she'd been studying too much. No sleep and ten pots of coffee. Wanted to sleep, needed to sleep, couldn't sleep. It was a terrible feeling, with little shadowy hallucinations dancing at the periphery of her vision and little twitching muscle contractions starting up in her legs and eyelids.

She needed to sleep. She needed a break from the relentless worry. The raging guilt. Curled up with Lorenzo, perhaps she could doze off for a while.

Without modesty, she stripped off her clothes and climbed into the soft, warm bed. In a moment, he was with her, his long arms around her. She snuggled down, her head on his shoulder, his masculine, vague motorcycle scent infiltrating her pillow, his soothing aura enveloping her.

But her muscles continued to tense up. She had to consciously tell herself to relax a couple of times. Her muscles would relax, and a moment later, she was clicking her teeth together again in some impatient rhythm.

Nicky. Where was he? What was he doing? Were they manhandling him? Were they hurting him? Would she see him again soon?

Then she relaxed, took some deep breaths, and fell softly into sleep, waking briefly when Lorenzo began to snore.

*Life is never perfect,* she thought. *I finally find the perfect man and the rest of my reasonably sane life explodes.* She snuggled down closer, kissing and tasting the skin on his chest.

In his sleep, he rubbed his chin on the top of her head and pulled her to him, nesting one long leg between her two, and pulling it up to rest comfortably in her crotch.

*The perfect man,* she thought, *the perfect man for me.* With that thought, Sweetann snuggled closer to the man of her dreams and relinquished her hold on everything else.

# Chapter 32

"Natalie? Natalie, wake up."

Richard started shaking his wife and did not stop until she opened her eyes, batted wildly at his arms, moaned and choked and then sat up. "What!"

"We've got to go."

She reached for the nightstand, and Richard's heart sank. Again. The heroin was no longer there, but that was her first waking thought. Not of him, not of where they were or where they were going, but for the dope.

Before she had her eyes open, even.

He thought maybe it would be a good idea to slip his wedding ring around a rolled up baggie of the stuff and let her live with it instead. He thought of just leaving her here. She could figure it all out later.

But now she was awake, if not aware, and he needed to get to the airport, so she needed to get her shit together.

He got her up and moving, though she moved slowly and was prone to stop and cock her head as if listening to instructions from another dimension. When she did that, he had to jiggle her to get her to return to present time and space.

Just as she was straightened around, dressed in a wrinkled mess of clothes, her face washed and mannequin-pale with no makeup, the heaves hit her and she spent ten minutes over the toilet bowl.

Richard didn't have the patience to hold her head, smooth her hair or speak low words of love and support.

He called the front desk to arrange for a rental car, and the clerk said, "Is everything all right up there?"

"Everything's fine," Richard said.

"Are you checking out?"

"Yes, we'll be checking out. Soon."

"I'll have to charge you for today."

"Yes, of course, I'll be in to settle up. Please just ask someone to deliver us a rental car. Compact. Cheap. Just for one day. Now. Soon."

"I'll see what I can do," the clerk said, and disconnected.

Richard sat at the little desk, thumbing through the Best Western Worldwide Directory and waited. When Natalie had been quiet for a while, he went in to the bathroom to check on her.

She was sitting on the floor, her cheek on the toilet seat, exactly the way Richard had seen lots of his college roommates sit after a long night of tequila.

"C'mon, Natalie, rinse your mouth," he said, feeling merciless and mean. He'd just been beat up on by Boingo, the little thug, and now he had only his stupid wife to take it out on. He was pissed off that he'd gotten himself into this situation, and pissed off that this was the only way to get out of it.

"*Come on,*" he said, bouncing her a few times, "let's go."

She whined and growled at him, but he was in charge for a change, and she obeyed. Letting him lift her from the floor, she steadied herself with one hand on the vanity.

She looked at herself in the mirror and grimaced.

"Get my cosmetic bag," she said.

"No time."

"I'm not leaving without makeup on," she said, then clung to the sink with hawklike fingers while she closed her eyes. Richard watched the blood drain from her face again.

Richard fetched her cosmetic case and set it on the closed toilet lid. She opened her eyes, and slowly brushed her teeth, then brushed her hair and tied it back with an elastic band. She washed her face with the little bar of motel soap, rinsed it, then slathered on a moisturizer. She moved in slow motion, and it took all the control Richard had to keep from yelling at her, or grabbing her arm and jerking her right the hell out.

Her hand wasn't steady enough to apply any real makeup. He watched her swipe on a little eye shadow, then streaked on some foundation to mask the dark circles under her eyes. She still looked bad. She looked real bad.

"I need a drink," she said.

"I bet you do," Richard answered. "But we have to go to the airport, so a drink is out of the question. Unless you want me to drop you off at a bar and pick you up later."

"Airport, oh yeah. Well, I can get a drink there." Natalie tried desperately not to show that she didn't know what was going on.

Airport.

Someone coming in? Someone leaving?

Was it Sunday night, and they were taking Sweetann to the airport so she could go home?

Where the hell was Sweetann anyway? She felt her heart want to pump with anxiety, but it didn't have the energy.

"Yeah," Richard said, disgusted beyond words. "You can get a drink there. You can get lots of drinks there." *And maybe you can just fucking stay there and die*, he wanted to add, but didn't.

He saw the confusion in her eyes as she looked from his hardened reflection back to her own ravaged one.

She had no idea what was going on. Just as well, he thought, took her hand, and led her out of the motel room.

# Chapter 33

The Cook awoke instantly alert, as always. He stretched long and hard, his lean body feeling cool and smooth against the white sheets. A soft breeze blew across him from the French doors he had opened a crack before he went to sleep. It funneled the air conditioning over him just right.

He looked at the clock. A perfect one-hour nap.

He showered, shaved, changed into a fresh shirt, tie and suit, then went to the kitchen.

Felicia was talking to the housekeeper, wearing only her bikini bottoms and a towel across her shoulders.

"You're going out again?" she asked when she saw him.

"Gotta pick someone up at the airport."

"Hungry?"

"Yeah." He poured himself a cup of coffee from the perpetual pot and sat on a stool at the counter while the housekeeper hustled around making him a sandwich.

Felicia sat beside him. She smelled earthy, like suntan oil and hot skin. "Get cleaned up and put some clothes on," he said to her.

She looked up at him in surprise. "Why, am I going with you?"

"No, I just don't want you walking around the house like that. You look like a slut."

With her eyes on him in a steady, undecipherable gaze, she got off the stool, turned and walked down the hall. In a moment, he heard the shower going. Another moment, and he was biting into a crunchy cucumber and cream cheese sandwich.

This airport thing, he thought. This is going to be tricky.

## Chapter 34

Boingo got to the airport way too early. He was itchy and twitchy after his goddamned wild goose chase to the hospital, looking for Richard and his bitch wife, and he was so pissed off he didn't know what to do with himself. God *damn* them, anyway. God *damn!*

He told the guy he was with to drive around the terminal for a few hours, or park it, or take in a movie or something. He didn't know what. He'd call when he had the kid. If he ever got the kid. He didn't know what this kid looked like, he didn't know what airline he was coming in on, he didn't even know what terminal at LAX. He only knew that if he didn't get this kid and get this dope for Mr. Hunter, his life was over.

He looked at the incoming flight monitors and didn't see any 6:40 flights from Seattle. He wondered if it was coming in from Salt Lake City or something. Reno, maybe.

Oh, shit, he was looking at the monitor for departing flights. What an idiot.

Las Vegas.

There was a flight leaving for Las Vegas soon.

He looked at his watch. He was so early, he could hop a shuttle to Vegas, spend an hour or so at the tables—they even had a casino at the airport, didn't they? Then hop on back and *still* be in time to greet the kid on the 6:40.

Nothing settled twitchiness like a pocketful of cash.

And Boingo was feeling lucky today, for some reason. Maybe it was seeing his old friend Lorenzo, cleaned up and looking healthy. Maybe it was the break Mr. Hunter was giving him. Maybe it was the woody in his shorts when he thought about a quickie with Las Vegas. Whatever it was, it was not to be denied. Lady Luck smiled irregularly upon Boingo, but he could feel her toothy grin twinkling down on him right this very second.

In spite of Richard and his stupid wife.

Somewhere, a poker room was calling to him, and he knew that if he had a good time at the table, he could pay back Mr.

Hunter and never have to worry about performing these little trained-dog tricks for him ever again.

He checked the departure monitor again.

He had no luggage; he could make his reservation and check in right here, right now on his phone.

If he ran, he could just catch the next flight.

# Chapter 35

In his dream, Lorenzo was driving the BMW down a quiet, tree-lined street. The window was open, a scented breeze blew across his face. He adjusted his sunglasses, then looked down to tune the radio. He looked up just to see Sweetann, her son in tow, step out into the street, right in front of the car.

They made eye contact, horror on both their faces, as he slammed on the brake—

Lorenzo's leg kicked out and woke him up. His heart pounded.

Sweetann made a little sound and turned over, curled up into herself.

"Jesus," he breathed. Was that what he was doing? Was he about to slam right into Sweetann and Nicky's life and leave them dead by the side of his road?

Was he still on that path to self-destruction? Had getting clean and sober meant nothing?

His mouth tasted gritty, his stomach felt upset.

He slipped out of bed, pulled on his leather pants and went to the bathroom.

He looked at himself in the mirror, brushed his teeth with somebody's toothbrush, then thought about all that dope in the trunk of the Beamer.

He stood in the doorway of the bedroom for a long time, watching Sweetann sleep. He was about to go outside and bring in that suitcase. He knew it. He didn't know why, and he didn't know what he was going to do with it, but he knew he was going to mess with that dope, and it was an act that he felt absolutely powerless to control.

He breathed deeply of the scent of lovemaking that filled the room, and the sound of her breathing, and he wished, he desperately wished things were different.

That he was different.

That circumstances were different.

He didn't deserve a woman like that.

He made a fist and whacked the doorjamb a couple of

times, just hard enough to hurt, but it didn't change anything.

He took the keys from the kitchen countertop and went outside.

He grabbed the black suitcase and the McDonald's bag and brought them both inside. He put the suitcase on the couch and opened it.

The little taped-over slice in the brick caught his attention and wouldn't let him go.

He watched his actions as if he was watching someone in a movie, and he was cringing in his seat, saying, "No, don't do it, don't do it," all the while knowing that the jerk on the screen was a tragic figure. He was going to throw away everything he had gained, including all his self-respect, in a matter of moments. For nothing.

For nothing.

Six years clean and sober felt like six years wasted, when he could have been enjoying himself instead.

*Was that right?*

Lorenzo stared at that open suitcase and stared at it while he took the other brick out of the fast food bag and nestled it in the suitcase with its brothers.

All he had to do was lift the little piece of tape that covered the slice in the brick. All he had to do was pull out a tiny taste and put it up his nose.

Then he would be different.

Sweetann and Nicky would be free of him, because he'd be back in prison. If not a literal prison, then a soul prison. And a brick-and-bars prison wouldn't be far behind, because he knew what he'd do. He knew how he'd get. It had happened too many times before to escape him now.

Fuck.

He wished Jack were around. His sponsor. Jack would talk him down from this in a heartbeat. But Jack was out of the country, and Lorenzo was in his house, with dope. He was already screwing over his friends, and he hadn't even tooted any of that magic powder yet.

He picked up the brick and set it up on the kitchen counter. He pulled up a stool and sat, staring at it.

He wanted to smell it. He wanted to lick it. He wanted to

fondle it, rub his hands over the smooth wrapping. Maybe he'd get some of the powder on his finger tips, it would soak in, and he'd get high without actually having to do anything.

That square of packed powder was, absolutely, without a doubt, the most powerful, the most beautiful thing he had ever seen.

In the back of his mind, he knew he should put it away, lock the suitcase and go back to bed. He had a half dozen Narcotics Anonymous member's phone numbers memorized; he could just pick up the phone and let a little sanity in.

He was sitting with six kilos of heroin and was expecting someone to help him find some sanity in the situation?

Not likely.

The cellophane tape Natalie had put on had the little slice he'd cut into it was curled at the edge. It had been lifted several times and a little dirt had turned the edge black. It could be easily lifted.

He put a fingernail under it and lifted.

Some tan crystalline powder stuck to the tape in a thin line.

I should just lock this away, he said to himself, but his curiosity, or a residue of his addiction, or something, had him in its grip and he felt completely out of control.

It was compelling, this stuff. It was compelling as hell.

He looked at it and felt its power. It had been his god for so many years....

He opened the kitchen drawer and pulled out a steak knife. He slipped it inside the slit and pulled out a tiny taste of sparkling brownish powder.

He pushed the brick aside and set the knife on the counter. He looked at the heroin and knew for certain that it was going to go up his nose.

He tried to think the act through, like he had been hearing in six years of meetings.

*It is not the answer to any problem, it is only a complication.*

If he put this in his nose, he'd be putting it in his veins next.

Within the hour. Within the hour, he'd be back at this countertop, a fresh box of syringes from the pharmacy at his elbow, cooking this in one of his sponsor's spoons and injecting it into one of his scarred and damaged veins.

Then he'd sell Sweetann's son, he'd sell Sweetann, and he'd sell his soul to keep doing it.

He'd go to prison. He'd die a junkie's death, choking on his own vomit, pissing himself as he hid behind some dumpster somewhere.

"No," said the addict inside him, "It's just one taste. What could that hurt?"

*Can't have just one taste, Lorenzo. You're six years clean and sober. Six years clean. Remember how it was? Remember what it was like getting clean? Remember kicking in jail? Remember detox? The creepie-crawlies? The sweats? The bone-aching pain?*

*Remember the insanity?*

*That's what this is, Lorenzo, this is just the insanity. Rinse off that knife and go back to bed. Say a prayer. The insanity will go away, if you will fight it.*

*If you can outwait it.*

*The insanity is powerless. It is temporary. You are greater than it. And there is a power even greater than you who will help you.*

Sweetann.

Her taste, her smell, her touch came back to his mind.

She deserved so much more, someone so much better than him.

*You could be worthy, Lorenzo,* the voice of reason in his head said. *Just rinse that knife off and go back to bed.*

*Become worthy.*

He wet the tip of his finger and dipped it into the powder, then touched it to his tongue.

That taste.

It burned his tongue as if it were acid. He grabbed a paper napkin and tried to wipe it off his tongue, but he couldn't get rid of that taste.

Poison, that shit was poison, burning a hole through the skin on his tongue.

He jumped backwards off the stool, put the knife in the sink, ran hot water on it. He spit, spit again, then rinsed his mouth with hot water. That taste. That awful taste.

Holy shit.

That had been a very close call.

He sealed up the slit in the brick, put it back in the suitcase, closed it and set it by the door.

He went back to the kitchen, stuck his head under the faucet and rinsed off the sweat that had accumulated there during the battle that the devil on one shoulder had with the angel on the other shoulder.

Heroin on one shoulder and Sweetann on the other.

Then he dried his hair with a dishtowel, and went back to stand in the doorway of the bedroom, watching Sweetann sleep.

"Thank you God," he whispered. "Thank you God, thank you Jack, thank you every single junkie who has ever spoken in any NA or AA meeting."

He felt as if those six years of constant meetings had given him an insurance policy he didn't know he had, but when he needed to call on it, it was there. He hadn't thought it was, but it came through in the end.

Whew. What a rush.

That was the car wreck he'd just dreamed of. That was him almost slamming into Sweetann and her son at a speed that would have crushed them.

Close call didn't even begin to describe it. But it didn't happen. He didn't snort it. He didn't shoot it. He was still clean and sober. Six years clean and sober.

Maybe God was trying to tell him something. Maybe God had put this angel in his bed as a reward for six years of doing the right thing.

Then maybe he ought to keep doing the right thing and life would continue to be its own reward.

He laid down on the bed next to her warm body and breathed deeply of her warmth, of her life.

And for the briefest of moments, he got a glimpse of *their* life.

And it was good.

# Chapter 36

Nicky got back into his seat and buckled his seat belt without looking at William. He felt guilty, although he didn't know why; he didn't owe this guy anything. Still yet, he had sneaked around and was going to end up lying, and that wasn't right, no matter what.

But he was pretty sure it would be okay with his mom that he'd been sneaking around behind William's back, and lying to him, too. This was the guy who hurt Charlotte, maybe even killed her. His mom would forgive him this time.

He put on the headphones, flipped around through all the stupid music and finally settled back to country and western. He picked up the shopping catalog and went through it slowly, page by page, reading as much of the descriptions of the stupid things as he could stand. The waiting was making him crazy. It seemed like forever.

He just wanted to touch down on the ground and see his mom.

She'd be there, at the airport, wouldn't she?

Oh man, what if she wasn't?

He crumpled up a page of the catalog in his fist. He'd started something, and now he wasn't sure that he'd done the right thing.

*Well,* he said to himself, *you should have considered all the options, all the angles before you acted.* He could hear his mom's voice in his head.

*When you take the action, you accept the consequences.*

He smoothed out the catalog page and for a moment got lost in the cool electronics that were pictured there.

There was something else his mom always said, and that was that as long as he had his smarts, he'd do just fine in life.

*And that's just what this is. Life. Weird life, but life. And I have my smarts, although they don't always work.*

He looked over at William, who was also listening to some music, his hand drumming on his knee.

Nicky had a big smarts advantage over that one, for sure.

Yep, he'd set things in motion, and somehow, it would all work out. His mom trusted him, and if he trusted her judgment, he had to trust himself.

They'd find each other eventually. LA couldn't be that big, could it?

He just wanted the stupid plane to land.

# Chapter 37

When Sweetann woke up, Lorenzo had one of her breasts in his mouth, and he was treating it very nicely. She moved slightly to let him know he had her attention, and he looked up at her, his dark blue eyes clear and shining in the diffused light.

"Hi," he said.

She stretched, feeling feline and feminine. "Hi."

"Sleep well?"

"Um. Yeah. What time is it?"

"Plenty of time." He went back to that breast, and she felt the rest of her burst into anticipatory alert. What a great way to wake up.

She moved her hand down and found him hard, one tiny pearl of glistening readiness at the end of his smooth, beautiful penis.

With a move so natural, it seemed like they had been doing this for years, Lorenzo parted her with one moistened finger, then ever so slowly, with tiny, restrained thrusts, opened her the rest of the way.

A sudden, unexpected orgasm shook its way through her, and when it had passed, she looked up at Lorenzo with surprise.

He was smiling down on her. "God, you're beautiful," he said, then began to rock her again, as she wrapped her entirety about him—vagina, arms, legs, lips and love, and settled into the sweet joining of creative forces.

She wanted this man in her bed every night forever.

~ ~ ~

"No sleeping now," he said, and touched her lip with his finger.

"Go away," she said, but couldn't keep a straight face. "I'm a satisfied woman and I need my beauty sleep."

"Not a chance." Lorenzo plumped up his pillow and sat up against the headboard, then picked the telephone up from the nightstand. He got the number for the hospital, but no one by the name of Natalie Preston had been admitted or had been logged in to the emergency room. He called his apartment, but there were no messages on his machine.

Sweetann, soft and warm, turned on her side and laid her head on his thigh. Automatically, he stroked her head with his hand, surprised at how soft her hair was, at how small her head was compared to the size of his hand.

"No news," he said. "I guess we just get to the airport by six-forty." He tapped her on the forehead with a fingertip. "C'mon. It's time to get up."

She snaked around and took his soft penis in her mouth. He closed his eyes and smiled. There was no chance it was going to rejuvenate, and yet it felt so good. So good. So good that it did begin to rejuvenate. "Hey," he said. "Don't be starting something you can't finish."

She stopped, and he could feel her smiling, even though he couldn't see her face. "Okay," she said, "but only if you promise we can do this some more."

"Oh, I promise," he said. "I do promise that." He scooted down the bed, picked up her face and kissed her deeply and with something else that pulled on his insides. "I love making love with you," he whispered. Her arms slid around him, his legs wrapped around her and they lay there for a long moment, cheek to cheek, just breathing each other in.

"I had a dream," Sweetann said.

"Hmmm?" He fingered her delicate ear that had a tiny gold hoop through the lobe.

"We lived in Italy, and spoke Italian and ate crunchy bread and pasta and drank ouzo with dinner on the terrace every night."

"Ouzo?"

"Yeah, you know, that Italian stuff."

"Ouzo is Greek. You mean grappa."

"Whatever."

"You can do the drinking. I'll suck the flavor from your lips."

"In Italy?"

"Why not?" He held her quietly, tightly. "Wherever you want."

What a great dream. And she could have all the ouzo she wanted, if they could do this together every night, with Nicky in the next room and their baby in the bassinette. He almost thought he dared to deserve to have a dream as wonderful. He'd had a horrible near miss just moments earlier, and yet he'd done the right thing. Could he guarantee to this wonderful woman that he'd continue to do the right thing?

He didn't know.

Fuck.

He didn't know. He couldn't guarantee. She had to know that he couldn't guarantee anything. Nothing in life was for certain, he knew that, and she surely knew that by now, too, but there was a wild card in Lorenzo that she needed to know about before she sat down at his table.

He squinted his eyes against the pain of the curse that was going to follow him forever. He'd never be rid of the addiction. It was cunning, baffling, powerful, and it lurked in the dark corners of his mind, just waiting to catch him unawares.

No, that wasn't quite true.

The addiction was his lifetime companion, but it didn't have to call the shots.

Could he continue to do the right thing?

Yes, he could. He knew right from wrong.

He knew the right thing to do moment by moment, and all he had to do was to take the next indicated step in the right direction. And then the next step after that. And the one after that. One step at a time, one day at a time.

It suddenly all made sense.

For the first time, Lorenzo saw the panorama of his life as it could be, with kids and a dog playing in the yard as he mowed the grass and then relaxed in a hammock with a tall iced tea. He'd work and save and be respectable and retire and grow old with the love of a good woman, and their life would be a worthwhile, satisfying one. No more searching out The Big Score. No more slinking around corners when he saw someone he didn't want to face. Instead: All things in moderation. Savings account growing slowly but steadily. Mortgage decreasing slowly but steadily. Daily life progressing peacefully without trauma, without drama.

Other people did it.

Why had he never seen these potentials before?

Well, he had, he just thought it sounded boring. It sounded right for someone else, but never for someone like him.

Until now.

Until now, it was all about getting through the day, making another NA meeting, getting the next paycheck, dealing with the ugliness of his past, and paying only in cash because he couldn't be trusted with a checking account yet.

But the close call in the kitchen gave him a stepping stool to look up over the wall of the right-here, right-now and he saw the enormous range of possibilities.

He could do it. He could give himself to this woman and know in his heart that he would be the best he could be.

Damn. He was finally becoming an adult.

*Damn!*

He was suddenly eager to get rid of the dope and get Nicky and put all this drama behind them and get started on the new chapter.

He had a life to live, and he was determined to get started.

Slow down, cowboy. No jumping around. Not any more. Move slowly, move smart. Every day from now until the day you die.

He blew into Sweetann's hair. She could dream of ouzo in Italy if she wanted. He'd dream of a quiet night at home with the family.

The quickly-approaching appointment at the airport could be dangerous, could be devastating, and they both knew it. But for right now, they were simply holding each other.

"Okay," Sweetann said, and Lorenzo felt that they had transferred something between them, something soft and vulnerable that solidified into strength when exchanged. He believed that she somehow got his epiphany, too. They both felt it. And it was all the sweeter for him since he had almost thrown it all away in the kitchen less than an hour before. He kissed her cheek, kissed her nose, kissed her lips, and then they disentangled and jumped out of bed and into the shower.

Sweetann raised an eyebrow when she saw the suitcase in the living room, but she didn't say a word. Lorenzo loved her for that. He finished dressing, picked it up, took it outside and put it into the trunk.

"We'll grab Nicky, give those guys the suitcase, go get Natalie and Richard at the motel, and put an end to all this bullshit," Lorenzo said with a serious determination. He was finished with this, and he wanted the suitcase out of his life. Now. Forever.

Sweetann smiled at him. She trusted him, he could tell, but he saw a nervous line of tension on her forehead.

He knew it wasn't going to be that easy.

And she knew it, too.

# Chapter 38

Natalie didn't need to be psychic to know that Richard was mad. Furious. He drove too aggressively with a death grip on the rental car steering wheel, the muscles in his arms stood out in tension, he swore under his breath at other drivers. He tailgated everyone, dodged around in traffic, didn't speak to her, didn't look at her, didn't even acknowledge her presence.

She wished she were psychic. She wanted to know what was going on. But she was afraid to ask. She figured he was mad at her, and she couldn't blame him. It hadn't been a very good weekend. Not the first weekend she had ever lost, not by a long shot, but it had been a long time since she'd been loaded to the point of oblivion.

She was going to give up the booze and they were going to get themselves a baby, and whoops! There goes another weekend. She didn't blame Richard for being mad, but she had some kind of a weird wax-like film over her emotions, and nothing bothered her too much.

But boy oh boy, she'd sell her soul for a stiff scotch.

Soon, she promised herself. Soon they'd be at the airport, and if there's one thing that was in abundance at an airport, it was booze. She knew right where the bar was.

She assumed they were going to meet Sweetann and Lorenzo there, she assumed that Sweetann was going home. Natalie hoped Sweetann had good time. They didn't have a chance to do any shopping or any of the sister stuff she had sort of planned, or meant to plan, but a little adventure was good, and Sweetann probably had a lot of that, just in that 4x6 bed with Lorenzo.

Adventure. Suitcase. Dope. Money.

*That kid in the ski mask.*

Natalie began to hyperventilate as the memories slammed back. She held on to her stomach.

"You all right?" Richard spoke for the first time.

Natalie didn't know how to answer him. She didn't know if she was going to be all right or not.

She fumbled in her purse for a tissue and held it to her lips.

*I can get through this,* she thought. *I can get through this just like I've gotten through everything else.*

She adjusted the uncomfortable seat back and reclined a bit with her eyes closed and her head against the door. She'd just wait until they got to the airport. She'd find the first bar, belt down a couple of double scotches and then she could deal with whatever came her way. She could deal with anything then.

Anything.

With a couple of drinks, she knew she'd even be able to handle the memories of the smooth, cold gunmetal in her hand, the boom of the pistol, and the kid's brains on her wall and his blood soaking into her nice, beige carpeting.

The heated, disdainful atmosphere continued to permeate the car, emanating from Richard's space, but Natalie didn't care. A good scotch or two and she might just tell Richard to take a hike. He could have the house, stained carpet and all. Natalie would take the credit cards and get out of his life.

*Before she went to prison.*

She felt a trembling begin in her hands, even though they were lying quietly in her lap. She tucked them between her knees. That trembling could become trouble.

She kept her eyes closed, kept her head down, kept her hands still until Richard pulled up in the loading zone.

"Get out," he said. "And I'll go park."

She opened the door and fell more than stepped out. She regained her balance, stood up straight and tall, wondered what the hell she looked like, and walked through the automatic doors.

Stepping around bewildered people loaded down with baggage, she made her way past the ticket counters and found the small, busy restaurant with a cocktail lounge. Perfect.

She slipped up onto a stool and mustered up a hundred dollar bill and a smile for the bartender.

## Chapter 39

Richard knew exactly where to find Natalie when he was ready for her, if he would ever be ready for her again. He knew it would be best just to stash her away where she couldn't cause any trouble while this whole thing happened, and a bar was perfect. She'd stay put until he came for her. She was unpredictable in a crisis, but perfectly predictable in a bar. She was comfortable in a bar. Totally at home.

He drove around and around the stupid high rise parking lot, looking for a space. He kept checking his watch. It was 6:30 when he found a spot, took note of where it was, pocketed the keys and ran for the closest terminal.

He found the video monitor, found the flight number, and ran for the gate, only to be stopped by security. They wouldn't let him get to the gate without a boarding pass.

He had to wait by the baggage claim.

# Chapter 40

Charles checked his watch. At 6:30, he calmly put the bookmark in his paperback, tipped the dead cigarette butt over on top of its long ash and pushed the ashtray away from him. He folded his hands on the table in front of him, and closed his eyes.

Someone broke a rack of pool balls, and the sound cracked brittle and cold.

*Ten minutes*, Charles thought. *For ten solid minutes, while the boy's plane is landing, I'll think about Lorenzo's offer and Arizona.*

He tried to visualize himself poolside, under the shade of some brightly colored umbrella, with abundant wet bikinis stuffed full of firm young flesh ringing the pool. They'd be talking, kicking their feet in the water, their tanned legs looking good all the way to their perfect toes. He'd lie on a chaise lounge, sipping iced Amaratto coffee—no, make that iced tea Arnold Palmer style, with lemonade in it—and talking politics or philosophy with someone, watching girls prance around, their nipples hard behind their wet bathing suit tops.

He couldn't see the scene; it all looked like a magazine ad. He couldn't visualize himself there.

Not Arizona.

If he saw himself in Arizona at all, he saw himself in a bar, just like this one, air conditioned, dark, smelling like mold and old beer, smoking and drinking coffee and reading paperback novels.

There were a few changes he intended make to his life, though. He wouldn't die sitting in this booth, that was for sure.

But it wouldn't be Arizona.

Charles opened his eyes and looked around. Everything was the same as it had always been.

He lit a cigarette, took his one and only deep drag from it, then set it in the ashtray to burn down.

Everything was the same, but it didn't have to be.

*He* didn't have to be the same.

Somebody in the other room gave a victory shout as he

pocketed a bank shot, and Charles smiled.

That's what he needed to do. Pocket a bank shot.

He'd already taken his shot. It was now time to see if it banked, sank sweetly into the pocket, and paid off.

He checked his watch.

# Chapter 41

Lorenzo pulled up in front of the baggage claim area and turned on the BMW's flashing hazard lights.

"This is a tow away zone," Sweetann said. "You can't park here."

"Just for a little while?" They were late already. Lorenzo didn't want to try to find parking place. He'd have to park a mile away, literally a mile away and take a shuttle back.

"No, security won't let you park unless you're picking somebody up who's waiting to load their luggage."

"So they'll give us a ticket."

"Jeez, how long has it been since you've been at an airport? They won't give you a ticket. They'll tow the car away. Think about it," Sweetann said, and Lorenzo remembered that the trunk was full of cash and heroin. He certainly didn't want to have the car towed away.

"We need the car," he said. "We need the stuff to trade."

"Duh," Sweetann said, and gave him a wry grin. "You stay here with the car. I'll go get Nicky. If you need to, drive around the circle a few times, but I'll meet you right back here, in front of this baggage claim."

Lorenzo looked around in a panic, trying to figure out where he was. "Okay," he said, then Sweetann jumped out of the car and ran inside.

The moment the automatic doors closed behind her, Lorenzo felt a loss, a tremendous loss, a horrible, devastating loss, as if he was never going to see her again.

His stomach clenched against the sudden emotion, but then his attention was distracted by a black sedan that pulled in front of him.

The Cook got out, and looking fine in a lightweight gray suit, removed his sunglasses and entered the terminal.

The game was definitely afoot.

And Lorenzo was out of the loop, stuck babysitting the car and the goods.

The Cook hadn't seen him, but he would definitely meet

up with Sweetann inside.

Fuck.

He hoped she'd know how to handle herself with him. And with Nicky.

Lorenzo took a deep breath and tried to be calm his racing heart.

Just then, the security officer came by with her clipboard and indicated with a wave of her hand that he needed to move along. Slowly, he pulled away from the curb and started driving in circles.

# Chapter 42

At six o'clock, Boingo was up fifty-four hundred dollars and not about to quit. The dice were hot and they were with him all the way. Even at this time of the afternoon, women in gowns had him surrounded, smelling like diamonds, expensive perfume and easy sex.

He paid minimal attention to them. The woman he wanted on his arm right that moment was Lady Luck, and she was cooing into his ear. He knew that she was fickle, capricious, and inconsistent. He'd known her intoxicating presence many, many times before. He knew that if she saw somebody she liked better, she'd just release her grip on his elbow and walk to a different table. Alerted by the shout of victory, the tall, thin, expensive women would follow in her wake.

But right now, Luck had her hands in his underwear and was rubbing him just exactly the right way.

He blew on the dice, told her how lovely she looked tonight and threw them.

The crowd cheered and another five hundred dollars was added to his stack.

"Let it ride," he said, and gently checked to make sure she was still there before he threw again. Another few thousand and Boingo could go back to being respectable.

As soon as The Lady walked away, he'd quit. He'd not make the mistakes he'd made before.

Before, he'd been stupid and greedy. Not this time. This time he'd know when she was gone, and he'd pass the dice, take his winnings and go pay off a few debts. Or at least he'd make partial payments, and wait to hear her soft, seductive voice again.

He felt her come up behind him, grind her crotch into his butt. It was the best feeling in the world. He blew on those lucky dice and threw.

# Chapter 43

Seat backs were up, tray tables were locked in their upright positions, seat belts were fastened.

Nicky fidgeted. He tried to look out the window, but his seat was on the aisle and too far away. With great difficulty, he kept himself from stealing glances back down the aisle to the rear of the plane where he hoped his smiling flight attendant would be waiting and watching for him. He closed his eyes and leaned back, trying to visualize what would happen after the plane landed. He couldn't. He couldn't even imagine writing the next scene in this play. In this stupid movie.

At the sound of the landing gear being lowered, Nicky looked over at William. His face was white; his hands gripped the armrests so tightly that cords stood out in his arms. He was scared half to death.

Nicky smiled. What a jerk.

The ground came up, the plane floated on a rolling wave of air, then touched down.

Nicky flipped open his seatbelt, shouted to William, "I'm sick," got up and dashed toward the rear of the plane.

She was there, with a seat ready for him, just as she promised. The whole thing took maybe five seconds and he was buckled into a flight attendant's seat, out of William's sight.

The plane slowed. As it turned and began to taxi toward the terminal, Nicky saw his flight attendant come alert, her attention on the main cabin. "Please take your seat," she said, and he knew she was talking to William. "Sir, you'll have to sit down and buckle your... sir, please sit down and buckle your seat belt until the plane comes to a complete... sir..." She picked up a black telephone, whispered urgently into it, and the plane braked to a halt.

She unbuckled her harness, while Nicky cringed. She stood up and walked up the aisle. He could hear her professional voice. "The plane will not move again until you are in your seat and your seat belt is fastened."

Nicky heard William say something back to her, then he

heard a passenger yell, "Sit down, asshole."

A moment later, she was back in her seat, her face flushed. She whispered again into the phone, and gave a smirky look to another flight attendant. The plane began to move. She didn't look at Nicky, and he knew that William was watching her.

Then, of course, when the plane did stop, the aisle was clogged. No way could William get back to him. He was safe until they got off the plane, but William would be waiting for them at the door, wouldn't he? Then what?

Nick tried not to think about it. He just looked at the beautiful flight attendant and hoped she had a plan. He could take care of himself once he got out of William's way, but he needed her help to do that.

"Stay here with me," she said to him. "Someone is waiting to pick you up."

*Mom.*

Nicky smiled and relaxed. Mom always knew the right thing to do.

They were the last two off the plane. Nicky's heart pounded as they stepped out of the plane, but instead of going all the way up the little tube into the terminal, she opened the door by the tube's control panel and said, "Here, Nicky, follow me."

He went outside with her, down some rickety metal stairs, across the windy pavement and through another door into grungy place with a couple of old couches. Some guys in jumpsuits with headphones around their necks were drinking coffee.

A tall man in a light gray suit with slicked back hair waited for him.

"Nicky?" he said, and held out his hand. "Hi, son. Come on with me. Your mom's waiting."

The redheaded flight attendant smiled that California smile at him again, and despite the fact that this guy didn't look like the kind of man his mother would send for him, Nicky wanted to trust the flight attendant. This guy was no William, that's for sure, and probably not anybody William would know.

*What's the smart thing to do, Nick?* He heard his mother's voice.

He looked back up at the tall guy, who looked too smooth

to be real. He looked like a fake George Hamilton in that fake vampire movie.

Nicky hated being a kid with no choices. He shook the man's hand, then followed him out.

# Chapter 44

Richard waited at the bottom of the escalator while crowds of people who got off all the recent planes came down. Once at the bottom, they either headed for the baggage claim area or hugged and kissed their loved ones, accepted armloads of flowers and babies and cried and laughed and did all that stuff that he had no patience for today.

He waited and waited, and eventually, the flight attendants came down, pulling their little black suitcases, and then the flight deck crew came down, wearing their uniforms and pulling their big square valises and that was that.

There was one last guy who came down the escalator with a security officer.

"I'm telling you," the horse-faced guy said. "He was in the bathroom. A kid. A kid named Nicky. I was traveling with him. He never got off the plane."

*Nicky!*

"All the passengers have deplaned, sir," the security officer told him, and encouraged him toward the door.

"Not the kid," the guy insisted. "I think he might still be in the bathroom. He got sick just as we landed."

"We've been through the plane. The boy is not aboard."

"Someone talked to you, didn't they? The flight attendant? That blonde bitch?"

"The baggage claim area is over there, sir." The security officer pointed.

"I don't have any goddamned baggage," the guy yelled.

"If your traveling companion is missing, I suggest you contact the local police," the security guard said. "Please excuse me." He walked away, leaving the guy standing there looking as frustrated as Richard felt.

Richard looked the guy over. Flunky. Couldn't even keep track of a ten year-old kid. On a plane, for God's sake.

Somebody had taken Nicky out the back door. Nick was long gone, or else somebody would have been here to meet him and this jerk. Fuck. Somebody *had* been here to meet him.

Fuck, fuck!

Richard spun around. This had been nothing but a wild goose chase. He wondered why Boingo had sent him on a wild goose chase.

Because somebody had sent Boingo on one, that's why.

So here he was, standing useless at the airport. He had no dope, he had no Nicky, he didn't know where to find Boingo. He didn't know shit. He didn't know what to do.

He didn't understand any of this. He didn't understand why he was given the suitcase full of dope at the airport when his sister came in. It was bad timing. He couldn't have picked up two suitcases without answering a lot of questions. He had no idea the one Boingo sent him to fetch was full of money and dope. He didn't know what he was supposed to do with it, but apparently he hadn't done the right thing. He didn't know who Boingo worked for, or what the whole situation was about. He had no idea.

All he knew was that Boingo had caught him in a compromising position one time, and he owed Boingo a favor to keep that dirty little secret to himself. That secret was soon to become a moot point, but the general knowledge of what he'd done had to be released on his timetable, not Boingo's.

The next thing that happened was a little call from Boingo, calling in that favor.

Picking up the goddamned suitcase.

But now, he and Boingo were square, and that was for certain. He'd done two things for Boingo with faulty information, and neither had turned out well. There would be no more dealings with Boingo.

Richard didn't know what to do next.

Pick up his wife, he guessed.

# Chapter 45

Sweetann jumped into the BMW, surprising Lorenzo, who had paused at the baggage claim curb for the ten seconds the security woman was going to let him sit there.

"The Cook's got Nicky," she said, "and they're going to come up behind us any minute." She ducked down. He followed her example, sliding down in the seat. "There!" she pointed at the black sedan. "Follow them." She was out of breath, and her throat hurt from the long sprint back.

Lorenzo put the BMW into gear, let one taxi pass to act as buffer, then smoothly pulled out behind it. The Cook and Nicky were in the back seat. Two of Cookie's goons were in the front.

All the times Sweetann wished she had been born with the genes to be tall and blonde and striking looking were erased at that one moment when her average looks and average build were easily lost in the crowd. The Cook happened by when she was headed for the incoming flights monitor, to see which flight Nicky would be on, and his gaze never settled on her even once.

The Cook was the tall, distinguished, striking looking person that people always noticed, which worked to Sweetann's advantage and The Cook's disadvantage this time.

He strode right past her, and she followed. But he didn't go to a gate; he met a ticket agent and went through a door behind the counter.

So Sweetann waited and fidgeted, hoping to God she was making the right decision, hoping she wasn't supposed to be at the gate, waiting for Nicky.

And she waited, trying to make herself small and even more inconspicuous. Waiting had never been so hard.

But her call was the right one, because eventually, the door opened again and The Cook walked out with Nicky, who followed obediently, that wonderful look of adventure on the little boy's face. He had the Mariner's shirt on that Sweetann bought him for his birthday ("Clothes? You bought me *clothes* for my birthday?"), and he followed along just as anybody would expect a ten year-old to do.

It was all Sweetann could do to keep from shouting his name and running to pick him up in a big hug and never ever let him get out of her sight again.

But if she did that, she was afraid that something terrible would happen to one or both of them.

Or to Lorenzo.

So she saw the car they were getting into, and she ran down the sidewalk, dodging luggage carts and oblivious smokers, all the way to Lorenzo, and now they were following Nicky, a discrete distance behind.

Thank God he was all right.

They were close now. They were about to end this whole ridiculous nightmare.

"You did good, babe," he said, and put a large hand on her knee.

Sweetann closed her eyes and took a couple of deep breaths. She'd done her stint, now let Lorenzo take over for a while, while she contemplated something weird.

The reason she saw The Cook, was that she stopped, dead in her tracks, as she was passing the airport bar.

Natalie was sitting at a table, drinking a scotch.

She looked like death.

Sweetann had stopped so suddenly that a family walking behind bumped right into her. She waited while they passed by her, then another small family stream of traffic had to go by before she could cross the concourse and ask Natalie what the hell she was doing there.

Before she could do that, The Cook strode by, swimming confidently through the stream of weary travelers toting and wheeling and carting great amounts of baggage.

Sweetann gave up on Natalie; that was a story she'd have to hear another time—if ever—and she focused all her attention on The Cook.

"I think they're going to the zoo," Lorenzo said.

Sweetann took a deep breath and tried to relax.

# Chapter 46

It took Boingo an hour to win fifty-nine hundred dollars; it took him barely ten minutes to lose it. And another minute to lose another five thousand on Mr. Hunter's account.

It happened so fast, he wasn't even aware it was happening until he looked down and the heady pile of chips that had been there was gone.

Vanished.

He signed for that other stack, but it looked thin, desperate, and he knew that The Lady had slithered across the room, where he heard shouts of triumph start up. The fresh stack was gone in less than sixty seconds.

Her desertion left him shaking, as always, and needy. He felt like beating somebody up. He felt like slapping somebody around. He felt like choking somebody, like gouging somebody, like hurting somebody bad.

Real bad.

He felt like hurting himself real bad.

Here he was in Vegas. It was past the time the kid was supposed to come in to LAX, and he was still here. He was another five thousand in debt and he'd dropped the ball for Mr. Hunter.

There was no way Mr. Hunter was going to cover his new debt, either, not if he couldn't get a grip on himself.

Richard. Maybe Richard had picked up where Boingo left off. Maybe Richard could take over the whole fucking operation, and Boingo could disappear somewhere deep in Mexico.

Boingo moved through the crowd to the street and fished through his pockets. Enough for a cab to the airport. Barely, if he stiffed the cabbie on the tip. Good thing he'd bought a round trip ticket. He'd get back and have to face the music.

Again.

As always.

But something was going to have to change, that was for certain. If he didn't do the changing, Mr. Hunter would do him the favor.

Head down, tail between his legs, mystified yet again by his behavior, Boingo headed home, hoping the plane would crash and he'd somehow be remembered as a tragic hero.

# Chapter 47

"What is this place?" Nicky asked. "This doesn't look like any zoo."

"It's what we call the zoo," The Cook said as they pulled up in the weedy parking lot and killed the headlights. "Come on in."

Nicky crossed his arms over his chest. "Where's my mom?"

"She'll be here."

"Why would she come to a place like this?" Nicky looked out the car window at the neighborhood of abandoned warehouses. Twilight threw deep shadows amongst the buildings and the whole thing looked like an old black and white movie from the TCM channel. "She doesn't even know about places like this."

"She's been here a few times in the last couple of days," The Cook said. "She knows you're coming, she'll be here for the trade."

"What trade?"

"My Mickey Mantle for her Hank Aaron," The Cook said. "Don't give me a hard time, kid. Come on."

The blonde kid who'd been driving unlocked the warehouse door, turned on the big overhead lights, and the three of them, along with the guy who'd been riding in the front seat, went inside. It was just a big, empty, dusty old warehouse.

"I hate this place," Nicky said, feeling safer, now that he was on the ground and there was space around him. No locked doors, no stinking van, no zip ties around his wrists.

He knew was the star of this scene, that whatever was going to happen was going to happen because he had arrived. He thought he ought to take advantage of his status, because it was sure to be temporary. He knew how to act like a star. "And I'm hungry. Can you send one of these dweebs out for a Big Mac and a Coke?"

"Hey—" the blonde kid said, but The Cook silenced him with a faint gesture. Then The Cook hooked a thumb, and the guy curled his lip at Nicky and headed for the door.

"Fries," Nicky called after him. "Large fries. And an apple

pie."

"There are chairs upstairs in the office," The Cook said. "Let's go up there."

Nicky didn't like The Cook following him up to that loft-like office, but maybe it would be cleaner. Maybe it would be a vantage point where he could look down and scope out the situation when his mom showed up. Maybe he could help save the day from up there. There was nothing to be done from ground level. The only ways out were the one metal door they came in through and a half dozen rolling metal bay doors that were probably rusted shut.

He just had to remember not to act like a little boy. He was the star of this show. It was all about him.

He stood a little taller, puffed out his chest just a little bit.

The office was cleaner than the downstairs, though not much. An old desk and a few metal gymnasium-type chairs were there. The Cook sat behind the desk in a squeaky chair on wheels. The lights in the office were fluorescent, and they flickered.

Nicky sat on one of the chairs and looked out the window into the warehouse below. The other dweeb was standing by the door. Vantage point, yes, but whether or not it had an advantage was yet to be determined.

"You ditched William pretty good," Nicky said.

The Cook smiled. "Now *there's* a dweeb," he said and they both laughed, but the laughter fell flat after a moment, and they went right back to silent wariness. Nicky sat down and let his legs swing back and forth.

"My mom is all right, isn't she?"

"Yeah," The Cook said with a cavalier wave of his hand. "She's great."

"Did she do something wrong?"

"Not wrong, exactly, something not quite smart."

"What?"

"She took something from me. Something I want back."

"So you took me."

The Cook nodded.

"Must be drugs," Nicky said.

"You're a smart kid," The Cook said.

Nicky wanted to talk about Charlotte, but he didn't. If this guy knew that William had hurt and maybe killed Charlotte while Nicky watched, things might go a lot differently. They knew he'd tell his mom, and that she'd take him to the police.

He didn't need to let on to this guy that they were going to do that. But as soon as he and his mom could get out of here, they'd go right to the police station and have someone look for Charlotte.

A car door slammed outside.

Nicky leaped out of his chair. "Food?" he asked.

"Your mom," The Cook said, and stood up, putting a restraining hand on Nick's shoulder. Nicky shrugged him off, but stood quietly next to him and they both watched out the big window as the guy down there opened the door.

# Chapter 48

"I hate it when you're like this," Natalie said.

"That makes us even," Richard said, "because you're driving me fucking nuts."

"I want to stop by the house."

"We can't."

"Where are we going in such a goddamned hurry?"

Richard wanted to just stop the car and dump her at the side of the road. He didn't know why he picked her up at the airport bar. He could have just left her there.

Should have.

He didn't know why he had married her, had danced to her extravagant tune all these years. He didn't know what had kept him from murdering her.

But it was about over. He just had to endure her for a little bit longer, then he would be forever free of her. Or so he hoped. He hoped he'd find Nicky at the zoo with Boingo, because he intended to let Boingo know that he was done with him, too, and he wanted to collect his share of that suitcase.

That suitcase was his ticket out, but Richard knew that putting all his eggs in Boingo's basket was pretty stupid, too. Boingo was a whore, loyal only to the next person who'd lay odds. Well, Richard was laying a few odds right now, as he drove with his snotty, drunken, smacked-out wife next to him.

Odds were that Boingo, or whoever he worked for, would screw him over. Odds were that he'd never get that money, he'd never make that score. Odds were that he'd never escape Natalie, he'd end up dying in bed next to her. Natalie, the woman with a liver like a scrambled egg, and the morals of a junkie.

What had he been thinking all these years?

He took a fresh grip on the steering wheel and pressed down harder on the accelerator.

# Chapter 49

The message icon on Boingo's cell phone showed up when his plane landed and he turned on the phone. He stared at it for a while, before he realized that he better grab this bull by the horns, because there would be no outrunning it.

"Mr. Hunter would like you to meet him at the zoo," the voice said on the message.

The zoo. Nothing good ever happened at the zoo, and if Mr. Hunter himself was going to be there, it was bad news indeed. Clearly, he already knew that Boingo had missed the kid, and by now he knew that Boingo had blown another five grand on his account.

This was not a rosy picture.

If Boingo had a wife to squeeze or children to kiss, he'd do it on his way to the zoo, because chances were, by the time he was finished there, he'd not have hands or lips that worked. If Mr. Hunter didn't erase his face immediately, then he'd put him on some job that would land him in prison for the rest of his natural life.

Which was about the same thing.

Boingo wanted to slap himself silly. Or maybe he'd slap somebody else.

Richard. Yeah, Richard, the stupid jerk with the hoity-toity wife. It would be good to slap Richard and have his wife stand by and watch.

But that would never happen, because just having that kind of wife gave Richard a sort of power over Boingo.

Boingo was a loser, always had been, always would be. He'd managed to avoid facing that fact head-on for a while, but no longer. So he sat quietly for a moment and faced it.

He could put a bullet in his brain. He could. He had the bullet.

Instead, he put the key in the ignition, and drove slowly out of the airport parking structure, headed for the zoo.

Someone else could have the pleasure of doing the thing with the bullet.

# Chapter 50

"Nicky!" Sweetann's eyes were drawn to that upstairs window like magnets.

"Mom!" His little face disappeared from the window, and as Sweetann ran toward the stairs, the office door opened and his little body tore down the steps so fast she was afraid he would fall, tumble and crack his head open on the dirty concrete floor.

But he didn't, and when he ran into her arms and hugged her around the waist, it was the best feeling in the world. She even picked him up, big boy that he was, and hugged him and kissed him and smelled his hair, and squeezed him so hard she could feel his little ribs give.

"I think they killed Charlotte," he whispered in her ear, and while that news caught on a snag in her gut, it didn't make her let loose of him, not for a moment.

"You okay?" she whispered back.

"Yeah. I don't like those guys."

"It's okay. Lorenzo's going to get us out of here." She set him down, and with his arms still wrapped around her waist, she turned him around.

Lorenzo stood by the doorway, the black suitcase standing silently at his feet. He smiled at Sweetann. He smiled at Nicky.

"Who's that?"

"Lorenzo," Sweetann said, proud to introduce her son to him. Lorenzo was a good man. She could introduce him to all of her family, all her friends. And she would, too, the sooner the better.

"I remember him," Nicky said. "Is he your boyfriend now?"

"Hmmm," she nodded. "Sorta. Maybe. Yeah, I think so."

The Cook cleared his throat from the top of the steps, and all eyes went to him.

But before he could speak, another car door slammed in the parking lot.

And then another.

Lorenzo picked up the suitcase and moved to a shadow. Sweetann grabbed the back of Nicky's shirt and dragged him backward toward a wall.

The door opened and the blonde kid walked in with a Burger King bag and a soft drink cup. He looked around, looked up at The Cook standing in the doorway of the upstairs office.

"Somebody else here?" The Cook asked.

"Yeah."

"Let 'em in," The Cook replied, "and give the boy his food."

The blonde kid pushed the door open again, and held it. Sweetann had no idea who was going to come through the door, and she didn't want to know. She looked at Lorenzo, who appeared calm, his hands folded in front of him, the suitcase— the vortex of this cyclone—quiet at his feet.

Boingo slammed the door open and walked through, strutting like a little banty rooster. He looked around like he owned the place, like Lorenzo and the blonde kid were his underlings. "Oh, you got me lunch?" he said and made a grab for the burger. The kid held it out of the way and pointed at Sweetann and Nicky. Sweetann felt the spotlight of Boingo's stare, though she tried to make herself and her son both invisible.

Then Boingo looked toward the office and saw The Cook standing on the stairs. "Hey, Cookie," Boingo said.

"Boingo," The Cook said, and started down. "You've been a bad boy."

The blonde boy walked over toward Nicky, who boldly reached out and snatched the bag of food and the drink, then Sweetann pulled him away, out of the kid's reach. The boy leered at Sweetann, who lowered her eyes. She didn't want to have to slap the smirk off his face. She needed to stay out of the spotlight. She'd leave if she could, but she wouldn't leave without Lorenzo, and he hadn't finished their business transaction yet.

Boingo's cocky swagger vanished as soon as The Cook spoke. Now he looked like a bad dog, about to be beaten. "Yeah, sorry about that."

"I'd like to hear your explanation for events, Boingo. I

asked you to do a couple of simple things, and none of them were accomplished, and now Mikey is dead and I hear you hit a bad streak in Vegas. I'd like to find out just exactly how the fuck that came to pass."

Another car door slammed outside, and another, and Boingo had a moment's reprieve as all eyes went to the door.

The Cook nodded and the blonde kid opened the door and held it open.

In came Richard and Natalie.

"Uncle Richard?" Nicky whispered.

Sweetann shrugged. *How did Richard know about this place? What the hell was going on here?*

"It's his fault," Boingo said, strode over to Richard and slugged him in the face.

Natalie screamed and Sweetann clutched Nicky even tighter. Nick dropped the soda, the top came off the cup and brown liquid splashed all the way to The Cook's shoes. The Cook frowned, but looked to Boingo instead of Nicky. Sweetann pulled her son even farther back, farther away from any violent activity. She wished they were in a position to just back out the door and get the hell out, but they were on the opposite side of things, and Lorenzo was clear across the big, echoing room.

Sweetann was surprised she didn't feel anything more about her brother getting popped in the nose. Whatever he'd done, she knew he deserved it.

Blood streamed out of Richard's nose. He held it, the blood gushing through his fingers, as he winced and tried to look around.

"Hey, hey," The Cook said. "Boingo. That was uncalled for. I think you should apologize."

"Apologize my ass—" Boingo said, but Sweetann saw Richard lunge for him, just as his back was turned.

She covered Nicky's mouth, as she could tell he was poised to yell out.

"You fucking ass!" Richard yelled, and jumped on top of Boingo's back. Richard started to hit him, and the next thing Sweetann knew, Boingo had a gun in his hand.

But Richard kicked it, and the gun skittered across the

floor and came to rest in front of Natalie's feet.

Sweetann pulled Nicky farther away.

With a nod, The Cook dispatched the blonde kid to get the gun, but Natalie beat him to it. She picked it up and started to wave it around like a lunatic. "I'll kill you all," she said. "You're all a bunch of goddamned criminals. I'll kill you all."

Richard and Boingo stopped fighting when the gun got loose. Richard had gotten in a couple of licks, because Boingo's eye was swelling. The shoulder of his shirt was full of Richard's blood, and both of them were breathing hard and sweating, standing apart, wary. Blood dripped off Richard's upper lip onto his shirt and the floor.

"Do it, you stupid bitch," Richard said to Natalie, his chest heaving. "Kill everybody. Then you can have the dope and you can have the money and you can go live your life of drugs and plastic surgery until you die. Should take about a week."

"Shut up!" she screeched, her voice echoing in the cavernous warehouse. She pointed the gun at him. "You just shut the fuck up. I know all about you. I know all about you and your whore. I've lived with it long enough, and now I'm going to kill you."

"Do it," Richard said, and took a step toward her. "Put me out of my fucking misery right now, and then I won't have to look at you another minute."

Natalie gasped, and her face twisted up in pain. Sweetann felt sorry for her somehow. "How could you want Felicia instead of me?" she asked. Her gun hand sagged.

"Felicia?" The Cook asked.

Sweetann couldn't help herself. "Put the gun down, Natalie, before someone gets hurt."

"She's everything you will never be," Richard said, taking another step toward her. "I've been meaning to tell you that I would never want to have children with you, Natalie. You're an old, worn out, alcoholic mess."

Natalie opened her mouth in shock.

"You should die of a heroin overdose."

"You bastard," she whispered.

She looked at the gun, waved it around wearily for a moment. Then she slowly brought it up to her temple.

"Oh, don't be so melodramatic," Richard said, but she

didn't listen.

She pulled the trigger.

The harsh sound slammed around the inside of the empty warehouse. Sweetann put her hands over Nicky's eyes, but it wasn't long before everybody had to look.

Natalie's blood and brains were all over the door and on the back wall. Her body lay on the ground, in a remarkably graceful pose. Black-red blood pooled underneath her blasted head and began to creep in a stream toward Lorenzo. He stepped away, pulling the suitcase with him.

Boingo was the next to move. He went over, picked up the gun, and pointed it at Richard. "You're nothing but a fuck up, Richard," he said. "You've fucked me up for the last time." He pointed the gun at Richard's knee and fired.

Richard screamed as his leg buckled and he went down.

"Enough!" The Cook said. "Give me the gun, Boingo."

Boingo walked over to The Cook and handed him the gun.

The Cook looked at Richard, writhing in pain on the floor. "My Felicia?" He couldn't seem to get his mind around that detail. "My wife, Felicia?"

"The very one," Boingo said. "Saw them with my own eyes."

"Shut up," The Cook said to Boingo. "When I want shit out of you, I'll squeeze your head."

Sweetann looked at Lorenzo, who looked back at her. He looked tired. He looked pale. She knew she must look the same. She desperately tried not to look at Natalie.

Her hand moved to Nicky's smooth cheek.

The Cook walked over to Richard. "Really, Richard." He planted a vicious kick to Richard's testicles.

Just as he did so, a car door slammed outside. The sound was almost lost in Richard's howl of pain.

All eyes went to the door. "Jesus Christ," The Cook said. "Who isn't here already?"

"William," Nicky whispered, and dropped the burger bag to hold on to his mom a little tighter. The Cook heard him and smirked. He nodded at the blonde kid, who went over and opened the door.

Sweetann saw Lorenzo pick up the suitcase, and her heart

thumped double time. He stepped between Natalie and Richard, negotiated the route without getting blood on his boots, and came directly to Sweetann and Nick. He put the suitcase down, and put an arm protectively around Sweetann.

She felt power with him standing by her, guarding her and Nick. She hugged her boy and tried to imagine a circle of light surrounding them, protecting them in this dark and horrible place.

"Family," she whispered. She felt the power of family. Not necessarily the family that she was given at birth, but real family. Her family.

# Chapter 51

Charles felt too old for this, but at last it was almost over. He had one more thing to do, and this was it. His heart was heavy, because he had a bad feeling about what he was going to find inside that warehouse. He knew it would be bad the minute Lorenzo came to him with the contents of that suitcase. In a business where he'd seen just about everything, Charles had still been astonished that this simple task got so out of control that Lorenzo—*Lorenzo!*—had come to him with the goods.

But in about ten minutes, it was all going to be over. A lifetime of crap, and soon he was going to be done with it all.

The door opened in the side of the building, and a shaft of weak light fell out onto the cement parking lot.

Charles got his first glimpse of what he was afraid he'd find.

Blood dripped down the inside of the door, and a body lay just inside the warehouse. *Oh, Cook*, he thought, and his heart tore.

He entered the vast building and looked around. It was a woman's body on the ground. Richard's wife.

Richard, with a bloody leg, was holding his crotch and writhing on the floor not too far from her. Lorenzo and his two were next to the wall, and it looked as though Cook and Boingo were just about to square off before Charles had interrupted them.

"What a mess," he said to The Cook. He shook his head. "What a big, fucking mess."

"What are you doing here, Dad?" The Cook asked.

"Dad?" Lorenzo said.

"Dad?" Boingo said.

"Just checking up on things, Cookie," Charles said. "How the hell did all this happen?"

"It's his fault," Boingo said, and pointed at Richard, bleeding on the ground. "It's all his fucking fault, Mr. Hunter."

"Mr. Hunter?" Lorenzo said.

Charles looked to Lorenzo, wrapped around that wholesome

looking girl with her son. At least they didn't get bloody. "Get out of here, Lorenzo. Take your sweet girl and little boy, and take the money, too. You've acted with more integrity than all the rest of these hoons put together."

Lorenzo made no move toward the door. Good for him, Charles thought. He's going to see this project to completion. He wants to know the punch line.

"I'm retiring," Charles announced. "I've got a one-way ticket to someplace warm and a nice, fat, offshore savings account."

"*You* orchestrated all this?" The Cook asked.

"Puppets need a master," Charles said. "I'm just sick to fucking death at the way you all acted. Every one of you."

"You're you, The Cook, and the airport guys, too?" Lorenzo smiled at Charles with what looked like admiration.

A little respect was a nice touch for his retirement celebration, Charles thought. Thanks, Lorenzo.

"There are no airport guys."

"No airport guys?" Clearly astonished, The Cook was recalculating his life's work, always trying to best the airport guys, always trying to beat them at their game.

It was all a sham.

"I just invented a little competition for you, Cookie. You needed someone to work against. The guys at the airport work for me, too. Think of them as your cousins. And this last little task was merely to see if you've learned anything in your apprenticeship," Charles said. "Because it's all yours now." He looked at his son with tremendous disillusionment. "You haven't learned much."

He walked over to his son, to whom appearances mattered more than honor, and put his hand on The Cook's arm. "Here's what bothers me, Cookie. When I'm no longer the puppet master, somebody else will come assume the role. If it isn't going to be you, son, who will it be?"

The Cook looked like he was about to speak, but Charles held up his hand. He wasn't interested in hearing anything Cook had to say. No matter what he thought, he didn't have the macadamias to handle the business the way Charles had finessed it all these years. Too bad. Too fucking bad. Kids can be such a disappointment.

He turned his attention to Boingo.

Boingo looked contrite, but it wasn't enough. "I'm forgiving you all your debts, Boingo. Even the new five thou. You and me, we're even, but somebody has to account for Mikey, and I'm afraid the police were tipped in your direction."

Boingo looked at the floor, nodding slowly.

Charles walked over to Richard, one hand on his balls, one hand holding his knee. "Richard? You and Felicia deserve each other. You're both stupid bitches." He looked up at The Cook. "You know she's no great loss, Cookie. You need someone more like—" he nodded in Sweetann's direction. "Someone who will make you a good home and give you a couple of babies. Change your tastes, pal. Your mother would roll over in her grave."

The Cook looked like he was ready to cry. Good.

"I'm going to take the dope," Charles said, and pointed at Lorenzo, who delivered the suitcase to him immediately. "I'll send it back where it came from."

Charles picked up the suitcase. "I asked you, Cook, to do a simple thing. Pick up a suitcase at the airport. That was all. And look what your incompetence has done." He gestured at Richard and Natalie on the ground. "Just look what happened because you were too good to pick up the suitcase, you had to ask chucklehead here—" he gestured at Boingo— "Who further delegated. Stupid. Stupid!"

His heart heavy, Charles started for the door.

"Hey, wait!" Nicky pulled away from Sweetann and ran toward the old man.

Charles stopped and looked down on the boy.

"What about Charlotte?"

"She's okay, kid," Charles said. "I never meant for her to get hurt. She did get hurt, but she'll be okay."

"William did it," Nicky said.

"William has been—shall we say—disciplined. I'm sorry."

The blonde kid, Cookie's flunky, opened the door for Charles, bloody doorknob and all, and held it open.

Charles took a last look around the warehouse, his gaze settling on his son. "Look to your soul, Cook. You're almost a thug. Don't be a thug." He pointed at Boingo. "He's a thug."

He pointed at Richard. "He's a thug wannabe. Clean yourself up." He stepped around Natalie's body, through the door into the night.

It was over. He was retired. Good. He was shed of his business, shed of his family, shed of everything except whiling away the rest of his days rereading John Saul novels and getting massaged by women who didn't speak English.

His heart felt heavy, but he knew that would pass.

He'd send Cook a Christmas card.

# Chapter 52

Nobody moved until they heard Charles drive away. Nobody knew who was in charge. Nobody knew what to do.

Lorenzo pulled the keys to the BMW out of his pocket and jangled them until he got Richard's attention, "I'll leave the keys on the front seat," he said. "We'll return the rental car."

He dug the keys to the rental out of Richard's pocket, grabbed Sweetann's hand, she grabbed Nicky's, and Lorenzo led them to the door, careful not to step in Natalie's juices. The blonde kid opened the door, and without leaving a fingerprint or a footprint, the three went out into the Los Angeles night.

Lorenzo opened the trunk of the BMW, took out the black plastic garbage bag full of money and threw it into the back seat of the rental car. He left the keys on the Beamer's front seat, then got into the Ford with Sweetann next to him and Nicky in the back seat.

"Buckle up," he said. "We can just leave this car at the airport, don't you think?" He drove carefully out of the parking lot and headed toward town.

Sweetann opened the glove compartment and pulled out the paperwork.

"What about Uncle Richard and Aunt Natalie?" Nicky asked from the back seat.

"There's nothing to be done about Aunt Natalie," Sweetann said, "and someone will call an ambulance for Uncle Richard. He'll be fine."

"What's this all about, Mom? What happened to you?"

"Lorenzo, could you please pull over?"

He did as he was told.

Sweetann jumped out, and then got into the back seat and held her son, who began to cry.

Lorenzo wanted to climb back there and let Sweetann hold him, too. Instead, he got the car back on the road, and headed for the closest nice hotel. They could all hold each other all night long, affirm life, think about love, and make all the hard decisions in the morning.

# Chapter 53

Nicky didn't know why he was crying. It was a baby thing to do, and he didn't want to be doing it, except that he couldn't help himself.

The mental image of his aunt's exploded head and uncle's shot-off knee was a horrific one, even worse than in the movies. He hated having that picture in his head, that smell in his nose.

He wiped at his eyes, hoping to wipe away the sight.

He liked Lorenzo, he liked the way Lorenzo looked at his mom, and he liked the way she looked back at him. Lorenzo looked like a biker guy superhero.

Mostly, Nick felt disappointed, as if he was supposed to be doing something else, only there wasn't anything else to do. He felt let down. He felt as though he'd been an adult for a while, and now his mom was back and he could relax. And she could relax because she had Lorenzo.

He knew that things had changed forever. Some things would never be the same for him or his mom.

He guessed that was good, although the way things had always been were never really that bad.

His mom smelled good, and she was soft, and having her hug him was the best thing in the world. He felt the words in her chest as she talked to Lorenzo, and then the car started moving again, but he couldn't hear what she said, and he didn't care where they were going. He just wanted Lorenzo to be his dad, and for them to all live happily ever after.

"My burger," he said, and his stomach growled as if in echo. He'd left the Burger King bag on the floor in the warehouse.

"We'll order room service," his mom said, and then she hugged him again, and began to whisper in his ear.

He wasn't certain, but he thought he heard the word "family," and the word "Disneyland" both in the same sentence.

## About the Author

Elizabeth Engstrom is a sought-after teacher and keynote speaker at writing conferences, conventions, and seminars around the world. She has a BA in Literature/Creative Writing, and an MA in Applied Theology, both from Marylhurst University. She lives in the Pacific Northwest with her fisherman-husband and their dog where she is on the board of directors for Wordcrafters in Eugene (www.wordcraftersineugene.org). She teaches the occasional writing class, puts her pen to use for social justice, and is always working on her next book. www.ElizabethEngstrom.com

# Books from IFD Publishing

## Paperbacks

**Novels:**
*Death is a Star* by Christina Lay
*Baggage Check* by Elizabeth Engstrom

**Nonfiction:**
*How to Write a Sizzling Sex Scene* by Elizabeth Engstrom
*The Surgeon's Mate: A Dismemoir* by Alan M. Clark

## EBooks

(You can find the following titles at most distribution points for all ereading platforms.)

**Novels:**
*York's Moon*, by Elizabeth Engstrom
*Beyond the Serpent's Heart*, by Eric Witchey
*Lizzie Borden*, by Elizabeth Engstrom
*A Parliament of Crows* by Alan M. Clark
*Lizard Wine*, by Elizabeth Engstrom
*Northwoods Chronicles: A Novel in Short Stories*, by Elizabeth Engstrom
*Siren Promised*, by Alan M. Clark and Jeremy Robert Johnson
*To Kill a Common Loon*, by Mitch Luckett
*The Man in the Loon*, by Mitch Luckett
*Jack the Ripper Victim Series: Of Thimble and Threat* by Alan M. Clark
*Jack the Ripper Victim Series: The Double Event* (includes two novels from the series: *Of Thimble and Threat* and *Say Anything But Your Prayers*) by Alan M. Clark
*Candyland*, by Elizabeth Engstrom
*The Blood of Father Time: Book 1, The New Cut*, by Alan M. Clark, Stephen C. Merritt & Lorelei Shannon
*The Blood of Father Time: Book 2, The Mystic Clan's Grand Plot*, by Alan M. Clark, Stephen C. Merritt & Lorelei Shannon

*How I Met My Alien Bitch Lover: Book 1 from the Sunny World In-quisition Daily Letter Archives*, by Eric Witchey
*Baggage Check*, by Elizabeth Engstrom
*Death is a Star*, by Christina Lay
*D. D. Murphry, Secret Policeman*, by Alan M. Clark and Elizabeth Massie
*Black Leather*, by Elizabeth Engstrom

**Novelettes:**
*The Tao of Flynn*, by Eric Witchey
*To Build a Boat, Listen to Trees*, by Eric Witchey

**Children's Illustrated:**
*The Christmas Thingy*, by F. Paul Wilson. Illustrated by Alan M. Clark

**Collections:**
*Suspicions*, by Elizabeth Engstrom
Short Fiction:
"Brittle Bones and Old Rope," by Alan M. Clark
"Crosley," by Elizabeth Engstrom
"The Apple Sniper," by Eric Witchey

**Nonfiction:**
*How to Write a Sizzling Sex Scene* by Elizabeth Engstrom

# Audio Books from Amazon and Audible.com

**Novels:**
*The Door That Faced West* by Alan M. Clark, read by Charles Hinckley
*Jack the Ripper Victim Series: Of Thimble and Threat* by Alan M. Clark, read by Alicia Rose
*Jack the Ripper Victim Series: Say Anything But Your Prayers* by Alan M. Clark, read by Alicia Rose
*Jack the Ripper Victim Series: The Double Event* by Alan M. Clark, read by Alicia Rose